THE CROWN OF SIGHT

A Tale of the Eternal Dream

By

David Van Dyke Stewart

©2019 David Van Dyke Stewart, all rights reserved. This work may not be reprinted, in whole or in part, for profit or not, without prior express written permission of the author.

This is a work of fiction. All characters and events portrayed herein are fictitious; any resemblance to actual people, living or dead, is purely coincidental.

Cover design by David Van Dyke Stewart

Author's Note

The Crown of Light represents another chapter in the ongoing saga of the Eternal Dream, but not the "next" chapter of the saga. Rather, it is a story from an earlier time that makes up part of the tapestry of legend, myth, history, and religion that creates the background for the characters in *Water of Awakening* and *Needle Ash*. For them, the siege of Pelanalda is like our Sulla at Athens, or perhaps even more like Thermopylae – part history, part myth.

As such, this novella is an entry in a different sort of series, what I'm calling the *Eternal Dream Legends*. This story will have significance for a few of the characters from the main series, particularly that strange outsider known as Thokar, but like the mainline entries, this novella has its own identity as well.

# The Crown of Sight

1

Katach sat brooding upon his throne, its carved surfaces gilded with the treasure of his many conquests. Its bulk was held aloft on a wooden stand by two ranks of slaves, who bore it upon two great logs that sat upon their shoulders. Images of demons and human suffering ran up and down the back and sides of the great chair, a baroque cacophony of wicked iconography, dedicated wholly to the lord that sat upon it. Despite the jagged textures, it was comfortable, for the seat and back were made of supple leather, tanned by the finest craftsmen in the Draesenith empire. When Katach entertained visitors – usually heads of state he intended to bring into his power and will – he was sure to describe the secret of this leather, that it was made from the skins of kings who had betrayed or defied him. And an ottoman, no less grotesque, was being made, he was sure to remind the wavering prince. The roof above the throne, of the same sort of material, he only described to his subordinates, for it was made of the skins of those who failed him due to the unforgivable sin of cowardice.

The king of the grey-skinned giants gazed across the barren field at the gates of Pelanalda, the impenetrable domain of Pelanel the Great, the lord of the Bastion Elves, keepers of the secrets of the Prim in the hazy chaos that marched to the city's back; they were guardians as well of an ancient relic that concerned Katach's god. The slaves that held aloft Katach's throne, hale sun-darkened men of the southern territories, did not fidget despite the wind that blew across the battleplane, which brought stinging dust to cling to their sweaty bodies. Katach could sit as if he were upon stone, time being his own.

"My Liege!"

Katach tore his eyes and wandering mind from the white walls and tall towers of Pelanalda to look upon his last and greatest general: Saren. Katach narrowed his eyes as he looked upon the lean Draesen that stood beside the throne.

"Speak, General."

"We have ravaged all the lands as far north and south as we dare tread-"

"Do you dare tread no further? Does your heart quake?"

Saren fixed his face grimly. "I lost good warriors trying to find a way through the mist."

"But not yourself, eh?" Katach smiled slightly. "You were ever a fox, Saren. Perhaps that is why you alone have survived this campaign. But you are not to play the fox with me, general."

"Of course, Lord." Saren bowed, his maroon cloak falling to the ground around him.

Katach looked again to the city. "The game is at last coming to a conclusion. How much will he pay for the last of his fertile land? How much will they quake when I snuff it out?"

"These are high elves, sire, not men. They will not starve out easily, nor will they count farmland of so much worth that they will surrender."

Katach grumbled. "If they were men I would already have the city under my heel and the king's head for a wine glass."

"Sire, have you considered that they can conjure what they need?"

"I have. You are brazen, Saren."

Saren nodded. "Who else lives to know your mind and provide council?"

"I can command the ghosts of your predecessors, if I wish. Do not make me expand my roof."

"Of course, Lord, I only meant that-"

"I know what you meant, fox. You are in my mercy, and not indispensable. Remember that."

"How could I forget?"

"How indeed, with thy wagging tongue?" Katach picked up a nearby cup. This one was not a skull, but was carved from a holy relic of ivory looted from men so pious that they died upon the altar to hide it. Katach smiled as he swished the wine and drained it. "Nobody will come to save Pelanel. We need only be patient. One of my virtues, and yours, Saren."

"Thank you, my lord."

"How fare the warriors?"

"Good spirits still, my lord, but their lusts will only be sated by old wine and fat whores for so long."

"The officers?"

"Keeping discipline as well as before, though we are short on good battlefield commanders. We have had a few too many lions, I fear."

"If it comes to a sacking, make sure the lions that remain have an opportunity to die gloriously."

"Even at the end of the campaign?"

"This will not be the last campaign, Saren. Those that survive will be all the better. Do not grow fat on me."

"I won't. But lord, I must confess again I am concerned about the army's capacity to remain loyal if the siege is to go on too much longer."

"Don't worry about loyalty, Saren. Loyalty I can command. Discipline is harder." Katach stood up and hopped off of the platform, landing on the moist earth with a dull thud. His cloak of black flapped in the wind. He stood a head taller than Saren, who took a hurried step back. "Have a scribe sent to my tent. One with impeccable handwriting who knows high elven."

"Yes, sire." Saren bowed and held the awkward position as Katach walked past him and started down the hill toward the camp. Impaled upon the battlements were two soldiers, still clinging to life, stakes protruding from their mouths, which oozed blood. At the bottom stood two human females with bowls, collecting the crimson life. Katach could not remember the crimes of the dying, but he smiled at their punishment anyway.

"Saren," the lord of the Draesenith Empire called back, finding his general a few paces behind him, giving him a wide distance though they walked to the same place. "Send the scribe later on. I am inclined to see to my own desires for the time."

"Of course, my lord."

2

Prince Darathel leaned over the table. His sword, made for his father's hands, banged against the ancient wood and he moved it behind him nervously. Covering the table was an immense map drawn on canvas. Ghostly glowing points and clouds hovered over the surface, indicating where the enemy was camped and where its soldiers moved. The lamp above, filled with the ethereal light of the Prim, flickered out for a few moments, dimming the relief of the castle and outer walls, leaving the blue-white of the enemy army on the map as the sole source of light in the room… or nearly so. Before the lamp sprang back to life, Darathel caught the gaze of Ared, a dark elf and long-time advisor to his father in the ways of war and magic. Alone of the figures in the room, his eyes glowed with inner light.

THE CROWN OF SIGHT

"We will need scouts soon," Ared said, his eyes fading back to a natural hue of blue as the lamp filled the space once again with warm light. "The enchantment on this map will fade like the rest without eyes that can see our enemy."

"I don't know if we can afford those eyes," Darathel said. "We've lost so many, just keeping the Draesenith where they are."

"Whether we can afford them or not, we will be blind soon," Ared said.

"Blindness to the enemy's movements should not be our primary concern," Faedra, the high mage of the court, said in her characteristic even and soft tone. "Our empty larders will soon no longer be hidden from the people."

"Could we forage for food in the Fay Lands?" said Mardrel, the head of the guard.

"Not unless you are willing to chance many hands to bring back..." Faedra's voice faded away. She smoothed her long hair and sighed, "probably nothing."

"I could go," Ared said. "But I might not return with enough food... or in any sort of time that we need."

"How long?" Darathel said. "And how much food could you bring back?"

Ared chuckled.

"How *much*," Darathel repeated.

"You lack the understanding of your father or Faedra," Ared said.

"He might return in months, or years, or moments," Faedra said. "He might forget why he went."

"I don't forget," Ared said. "But it's easy to get sidetracked in there."

"If we could create food in any other way, we would have," Faedra said. "Conjuring something that complex requires direct access to the Prim, not just a vague understanding of a few concepts."

"Yes, but the balance has shifted," Darathel said. "My father is clearly losing control." He flicked the lamp. The light within grew slightly. "The magic of the Fay isn't responding anymore."

"We'll need to evacuate, then," Mardrel said.

"And leave the Crown of Sight for Katach?" Darathel said.

"I didn't say that," Mardrel said.

Faedra shook her head. "If it leaves the city, all that we have built will-"

"Nevermind that. Where could we evacuate *to?*" Darathel said. "The Draesenith have us totally hemmed in." He ran his hand through the blue lights on the map. "It would be suicide."

"Suicide would be better than handing over the crown," Faedra said. "I suppose we could still evacuate into the Fay Lands. The Draesenith dare not follow us there."

"You make the Fay *sound* like suicide," Darathel said. "Or worse."

"It can be worse," Ared said. "If you die, you can return, yes? Even for the Draesenith, this is true. But if you are changed into something other than you are..." Ared shrugged. "Well, it may be the last option, either way."

"We can't take the crown in there," Darathel said.

"We could," Faedra said. "Though its power here in the world-that-is would be extinguished. But seeing as we are evacuating, that-"

"My father still bears it, and he will refuse to take it there," Darathel interrupted, holding up his hand.

Mardrel gritted his teeth and rubbed at his face. "Or we could negotiate surrender."

"I won't enslave our maidens to the grey skins," Darathel said. "Forget about surrender."

Mardrel took a steady breath. "Will that be for you to decide, my prince? If we throw open the portals to the west and tell our people to charge into the ever-shifting dream, do they not deserve the choice to be a slave?"

Darathel frowned. "I won't entertain it. We'll have to think of something different." The lamplight flickered, but remained on. He stared at it a moment. "I will go check on my father. The rest of you, start thinking."

"Thinking or not, I will have to lead a skirmish soon, lest we be blinded," Ared said.

"I'll do it," Mardrel said. "I now know the paths through the edge of the Fay from our secret entrance as well as you do. Besides, I have a feeling your council will be needed here."

"Fine," Darathel said, turning to the door. "Do it, captain."

"I will join you, my prince," Faedra said.

Darathel nodded to her and left the room with the high mage following close behind.

3

"What is there to sabotage, sir?"

Mardrel took his eye away from his telescope for a moment to look at Talel, who stood leaning against a charred tree trunk, his face wrapped against the chill of the fog that billowed perpetually from the Fay Lands close at hand.

"Much to sabotage," Mardrel replied, "but very little we have the capacity to affect." He handed the telescope to the scout and sat down on a nearby rock.

Talel brought the brass-barreled device to his eye. His grey cloak and gambeson made him blend in well with the tumbled stone and old ash of the burned-out grove, but he made a stark silhouette against the glow of the Fay. There, the trees grew of their own light, stretching in a golden green sheet behind the city. The fog that enveloped the raiding party picked up that light and the misty plain of Balara looked aflame in the failing light of day.

"They have sabotaged themselves, I think," Talel said after a time. "To spite us, they have burned what would be food for them as well. I see even the remaining livestock they have slaughtered without thought to their own hunger."

"Katach is no fool," Mardrel said. "He will have left the farms and fields to the east intact, knowing we cannot march through the valley to reach them when he holds the pass against us."

"My sister says otherwise," Talel said. "We went far afield with Ared a few weeks ago, miles beyond the encampment, and they have ravaged even the unsewn fields. These ahead of us were the last, and now they gone."

"You made it that far?"

"We can avoid being noticed if the eyes are few, or are busy."

Mardrel stood up and grumbled. "Dark elven magic."

"Yes. Tara and I have a knack for it, it seems." Talel handed the telescope back to Mardrel, who put it carefully in a satchel at his hip.

"The Draesenith are aware of his talents, then, since they are willing to burn the fields behind them," Mardrel said. "I don't think he is aware of our ability to conjure food, however, or surely he wouldn't be trying to wait us out."

"I was under the impression the enemy strategy was working," Talel said.

Mardrel closed an eye. "What have you heard, eh?"

Talel smiled and shrugged. "If the Prim were as accessible to the mages as the leadership says, we wouldn't be out on this sortie."

"We're keeping the map updated, that's all," Mardrel said.

"Then why check the fields? Each time we do this you survey more land. I'm beginning to think troop movements are merely incidental."

"Watch your tongue," Mardrel said. "I don't suffer insubordination, even if Ared does."

Talel bowed. "My apologies, sir. You are right. I have grown too casual keeping company with the dark elf."

"Apology accepted. Now, where is your sister?"

"Tara will be here soon, I'm sure," Talel said. "But keep in mind she too must tread at least a little through the Fay to bring her riders hither."

"Let's hope she loses no more time than us."

"She's already lost some, but I'm sure it is fine."

4

The hard heels of Darathel's boots echoed on the marble floor of the gallery – a floor made of hundreds of unique, mirror-smooth stones that no elf or man had ever laid. Beside him the diminutive form of Faedra slipped along, her soft slippers making only a rustling within her skirts. She had put her hood up, though whether it was out of fear or reverence, Darathel could not guess. He watched her hemline move along intricate stone grain, complex like wood, but infused with the chaos of time. Sun fell on it in great squares from the windows above, lighting hidden crystals in the matrix.

He picked his head up and looked between the great pillars. The paintings that had been made since the creation of Pelanalda stood out from the wall, which was beginning to feel faded. Darathel sighed as the details slipped over and out from his mind. He adjusted his baldric, taking it in a notch so his father's longsword would stop swinging and hitting his left calf.

"I am forgetting," he said softly. Ahead loomed the empty door, a black portal which he always dreaded.

"So am I," Faedra said. "But we won't forget each other."

"You speak fatalistically. Do you know something I don't?"

"Many things, my lord, but of the future, nothing."

Darathel stepped up to the door and held forth his hand. The darkness rippled like water, then faded, revealing a sun-lit room filled with furnishings. Darathel and Faedra stepped in. The dark curtain formed behind them. When it did, the room grew darker as well. A halo of light surrounded a bed on the far wall. As if seeing it for the first time, Darathel flinched, then walked toward it.

On the bed lay an elf, breathing slowly. His eyes were open, and he wore a grim expression, though he stared at nothing. Bedsheets covered him to his chest, but he wore no shirt. His head reclined on a pillow, and on his golden hair sat a detailed circlet of golden-white metal that glowed with its own light, illuminating the dark space.

"Can you hear me, father?" Darathel said.

The elf blinked, then looked at Darathel. His voice was clear and slow. "My son. It is good to see you. How long has it been?"

"A day."

"So little time. It felt like years."

"It might have been longer to you, King Pelanel," Faedra said.

The eyes of the elf in the bed turned to regard her. "Good that you brought Faedra. How are our stores?"

"Gone," Faedra said. "The Prim is growing more chaotic as well. Our ability to draw forth substance is failing."

"I am at my limit," Pelanel said.

"The castle…" Darathel looked down. "I don't quite have the words."

THE CROWN OF SIGHT

"It is losing itself," Pelanel said, nodding his head slightly. "I feared this. Even without the army that encamps outside our walls, I feared it might come to this, eventually."

"That you would lose your power?" Darathel said.

"That Midgard might not suffer us. That the truth of the *dim* races would rest on us – that all you make with your own will you are destined to unmake."

"Let me take up the crown, at least for a while, so that you can rest."

Pelanel closed his eyes. "It is not your burden."

"It wasn't always a burden to you."

Pelanel, his eyes still closed, frowned and shook his head. "No."

"What shall we do, then?"

"Your burden is to find a solution for our people. I cannot divide my mind. I must focus on the Prim and the city."

"Shall we go out and fight? Have a heroic last stand? Should I try to send messengers beyond to Alfheim?"

"Go," Pelanel said. "Return later. See to your own duty, my son."

Darathel looked sadly upon his father and placed a hand on the ancient elf's chest. He turned to leave, but found that his father gripped his wrist.

"Your mother… Send her." The king's eyes opened again, and were shimmering slightly with moisture.

"She's… not here."

"Oh… Yes, of course. Is Faedra here?"

"I'm still here, my lord," Faedra said.

"Good, you've returned," Pelanel said.

"Returned?" she said.

The king turned his head and smiled at her. "Take care of my little one."

"I shall," Faedra said, and forced a smile.

Pelanel closed his eyes. Faedra glanced at Darathel, then turned toward the darkened door.

5

Talel threw another knife. It slid its way through the armor of the Draesen, the enchanted edge slicing through the steel mail like it was paper. It stopped halfway into the grey-skin's neck. Dark blood erupted as he slid off of his horse, landing near the first scout Talel had killed, a human.

The elf looked over his shoulder and nodded. Mardrel padded up, his sword drawn. He was followed by the rest of the scouts, who bore bows and crossbows.

"So far, so good," Talel said to the captain.

Mardrel peered around the boulder, taking in the steep slope up to the enemy palisade, tracing the wooden fortifications with his eyes until they disappeared into the night.

"Do you think we can remain hidden?"

Talel nodded. "Well enough to get close, yes. The problem will be getting away."

"We have two horses now. Maybe that is enough."

"I wonder if Tara ever arrived at the first meeting point," Talel said.

"Don't trouble yourself with that now." Mardrel turned back. "Halda."

"Yes sir," said a tall and slender female, stepping past the other soldiers in a stoop.

"How close must you be to set fire to something?"

"It depends on what needs burning," Halda said. "If the Draesenith haven't bothered to daub their fortifications, we could stand quite a ways off. Perhaps a hundred paces."

"Good. You'll go with Talel on these two horses."

"Strange horses, sir?" Talel said.

THE CROWN OF SIGHT

"You can handle it, I'm sure. They are simple beasts," Mardrel said. "Get close enough to light up the gate, if you can. If it's too dangerous, just burn what you can reach."

"Sir," Talel said. "I'm afraid I'm developing a bad habit of questioning orders, but was this not to be a scouting mission?"

"I see a target of opportunity, and we have precious few of those. They've burned every bit of wood for miles and miles, even a small chip in their defenses could prove advantageous."

"Yes, sir," Talel said. "I'll keep myself and Halda as inconspicuous as possible."

"Good," Mardrel said, nodding. "I'll move the rest of the hands down the slope a ways. Bring the pursuit back through the boulders, and we'll take them out at range. That should make for us enough time to reach the outer limits of the Fay Fog."

Talel saluted. "Halda, with me."

Halda followed him closely, keeping her grey cloak wrapped tight around her. The horses of the scouts had stopped their immediate circling and stood placid beside their dead riders. Talel paused beside the beasts to check that the dead were in fact dead. Satisfied with their glassy-eyed stares, he approached one of the horses. It bucked slightly as he took the reins, but calmed as Halda touched its flank.

"A bit of folk magic," she said.

"Stay close to me. I have a bit of magic of my own."

They mounted up and rode parallel to the high slope, staying in the shadows far away from the fires that lit the palisade.

"Do you think we can get close enough to the front to damage the gate?" Halda said, just loud enough to cover the beat of the horses' hooves.

"I'm not going to bother," Talel said. "That's a fool's errand. We'll do the minimum the captain desires, but I'll not risk more."

"He *is* the captain."

"And short-sighted, for all his years. The Draesenith are well fed because they have a long and robust supply chain. More lumber will be easy for them to bring in."

"It will still take time. We could at least-"

"I proclaim it too dangerous for the chances of success," Talel said. "Do you really wish to risk your young life?"

"For my people, I would risk it."

Talel grumbled, then said. "Alright. We'll take a look."

They rode toward the east, where the hill that held the vast Draesenith camp came down to the level of the plain. The wooden fortifications, in the form of a parapet with great wooden spikes made of tree trunks, came far forward of the gate. Several riders bearing torches ambled about, and Talel slowed to a stop.

"This is as close as we can get," Talel said. "Do you still object?"

"No."

"Get ready to ride."

Halda nodded and raised her hands. The staff she held in her right hand glowed with an inner light as she spoke words to herself, in a chaotic language known only to her. The meaning was clear to Talel as a great wall of fire erupted on the palisade, shooting to the sky. Two men atop the parapet dove away, flames licking their clothes.

The fire died, revealing a nearly untouched wooden wall. Flames sprang from the grass around it, but the wood was unharmed.

"They must have daubed the individual logs," Talel said, trying to calm his restless horse.

"No," Halda said. She spoke again, and again flames burst from the ground. Again, they died back, remaining only on the dried grass on the shallow slope below the wooden fortifications. "They are not daubed," she said. "There is something altogether different protecting them. Something that refuses to acknowledge my magic."

"No time to ponder that," Talel said. "Away, now!"

Halda turned her horse and followed Talel as cries from the enemy scouts sounded above the din of the crackling grass fire. They were joined by more cavalry, and were soon gaining on the elves as they raced along the south side of the camp. Arrows flew from guards above, but fell far from the riders.

"Thank the dreamer for the dark!" Talel said, urging his horse forward. They headed up a slope and down another, slowing to work their way among treacherous rocks and boulders, which were difficult to see in the dusty moonlight. The sound of pursuit was growing louder.

Talel and Halda paused and turned back to see some twenty riders nearly set upon them. Where they had all gathered from, Talel could not guess, but as they approached the first ten were all hit with arrows.

"Fire at will!" came the shout of Mardrel.

Talel waved to Halda and she followed him up a narrow track, passing the other soldiers as they went.

"Here," Halda said, turning her horse about. Her voice rang out clearly in the night, and a wave of primordial magic flowed out from her, crashing upon the enemy cavalry like sea foam. Two of the riders fell, smoke streaming from their armor. Another fell moments later, his mount in a death throw. For the rest, the magic seemed to have little lasting effect, though the beasts all seemed disturbed by it. They turned against their masters' commands, giving the archers enough time to fire several more shots each.

The small cadre of riders quickly withdrew, a lone torch remaining lit among them.

"Quickly now," Mardrel said, and dashed up the western slope. The rest of the scouts followed. Halda and Talel quickly pulled their horses into line.

"My magic is failing," Halda said to Mardrel. "I am not sure if it is me, or something else, but I am of no more use here."

"Ride ahead to the Fay Fog," Mardrel said. "See if Tara's squad ever arrived. If they did, tell them to head back to the city immediately."

"Yes, sir," Halda said.

Talel let his horse slow to a trot as the rest of the scouts ran southwest, making as direct a line as possible for the safety of the border between the mundane world and the shifting dream of the Fay Lands. Behind them, they could hear the unmistakable sounds of cavalry assembling.

"They will overtake us," Mardrel said between labored breaths.

"I can break off and lead them away," Talel said.

"That won't work. We're just in for a hairy time. I didn't expect so many cavalrymen to be out and about."

"And I expected Halda to not be tapped, but here we are. At least our maps will show true for a while."

"More than that, if we can make it back," Mardrel said. He looked back and spied over a ridge a growing light. "Here!" he shouted, and directed the squad to an ashy and tumbled heap of stone. They followed him into cover and nocked arrows. Talel dismounted and loaded his crossbow. They waited for a long series of moments, but the enemy never appeared.

"What are they waiting for?" Talel whispered.

Mardrel stared at the glow over the hill for a few seconds. "They're waiting for their second squad to flank us." He turned to the side and fired his bow into the darkness. He heard a few muffled voices react.

THE CROWN OF SIGHT

"Turn!" He said, half-whispered and voiced harshly. Before the others could respond, dismounted enemy dragoons appeared around the stones and charred logs, firing crossbows and charging with spears high. Talel choked as two elves next to him fell, one with a quarrel in his eye, the other with a pilum broken in his collarbone.

The elves fired wildly. A melee quickly erupted as the dragoons closed the distance. Swords were drawn. Being a scouting party and only lightly armed and armored, as well as outnumbered by the dragoons, the elves were quickly put to the rout and fell back into a haphazard semi-circle around Mardrel. The scouts, despite this setback, were well-experienced, and their curved longswords proved efficacious once they were in a sort of formation. Most of the dragoons lacked shields and were forced to fight man to man, much to the advantage of the elves.

It was almost enough to hold the Draesen and human attackers, though to what end Talel could not guess. Mardrel pushed himself forward through the melee, swinging his sword in long, chaotic arcs that were nonetheless effective in pushing back the enemy. More dragoons appeared, these mounted, then the Draesenith cavalry finally appeared on the ridge, bearing torches and firing crossbows. Talel caught a bolt in his hip, not deep enough to pain him much, but two other elves were not so lucky and fell in bitter finality to the wet earth.

"Run for it!" Mardrel said; there was no real escape from the cavalry, and Talel guessed his commander knew as much.

Talel turned from his opponent to obey, but found the way west blocked, not by the enemy, but by a small contingent of light cavalry cloaked in long coats and draping grey cloaks. He recognized his twin sister Tara at the head and understood why nobody had noticed their approach

"Onto the horses now!" Tara called.

Mardrel did not bother repeating the order. The scouts jumped and scrambled onto the horses, or just clung to the tack and saddles, letting their feet drag as the elvish riders turned to flee.

"Did Halda find you?" Talel said, forgetting his stolen horse and climbing up behind his sister.

"*We* found *her*," Tara said. "Sorry for the delay. The Fay shifted under our feet, and it took days to find our way out."

"Days?"

"It felt like it. At least the enemy will have a hard time following us back in."

"He won't dare. We learned some things tonight, though it cost us dearly. I must speak to Ared immediately."

6

The scribe took a breath and wiped the sweat from his brow. He placed his pen back into the shallow inkwell, then held up the scroll, making sure his calligraphy fit his standards. The slant of every line was in perfect parallel, the termination of every letter razor-sharp. He could hear, almost feel, the breathing of Katach behind him.

"I'm impressed, Yami. You write well for a man who is so terrified," the emperor said.

Yami scratched his nose and stood up, presenting the scroll to Katach. "Should I not be terrified, my lord?"

Katach smiled as he took the scroll. "You should be. But I wonder how you can have every part of your body shake besides your hands and eyes."

"Practice, I suppose. It takes many years to perfect the art of calligraphy in my homeland. My teacher used to cut my knuckles each time I-"

"I don't care about your life story," Katach said, his voice smooth and even. He walked to the table and spread out the paper of the scroll. From the belt that held in the folds of his black robe he drew forth a dagger of a white silver sheen. He touched the palm of his left hand. Blood began to run down the blade, purple-black, and in a greater quantity than Yami would have guessed from such a small wound. Katach pressed his hand down on an empty space below the writing.

Yami gasped. The blood was oozing around Katach's palm and fingers, but was lifting itself from the surface of the paper like a dozen living tentacles, thrashing about and reaching for the edge of the page. Katach withdrew his hand and the blood continued to dance, then fell into a strange pattern, turning into bright gold leaf on the page.

"You have seen this before?" he said to the scribe.

"No," Yami said back. His voice almost faltered as he said, "But I know what it is."

"Good. You can deliver it to the king of the elves."

Yami felt acid burn his throat. "Me? *Me*?"

"Did I speak unclearly? Is there someone else here?"

"N-No, my lord, I was merely-"

"Merely a servant who does what he is told."

"Yes," Yami said.

"Obedient to a fault?" Katach rolled up the paper, but left it sitting on the table.

Yami looked up into Katach's cold, unreadable eyes. "Loyalty to you is not a fault, my lord."

Katach smiled. In a single quick motion, he grabbed Yami's hand and pricked it with the silver knife. Instinctively, Yami pulled back, but found the great bony hands of his master unshakeable. Katach pressed the scribes hand onto the outside of the scroll. Yami cried aloud in pain.

"Relax, scribe. You should know how to do that," Katach said.

The blood from Yami's hand danced like that of Katach, but did not settle in a pattern of gold. Instead, it went from bright red to black.

"Now you are bound to deliver this message," Katach said. "Go get a horse."

"Tha-Thank you, lord?" Yami said. He bowed and held the scroll close to himself. Holding the bow, he backed out of the room.

As the tent flap closed, Katach began laughing.

7

"This fat human is no army messenger," Ared said. His fingers danced along the cloth-wrapped hilt of his sword.

"Indeed," Yami said. "I am a scribe. Just a scribe."

"He has the fat of a scribe," Darathel said, though he did not look at the man. The prince held Yami's scroll in one hand, his eyes fixated on its strange seal: supple like wax, but resilient, revealing images if one looked away, and lines of magic when one studied it closely.

"It's a blood seal," Faedra said. "A way of compelling truth."

"Compelling?"

"Magic. It varies with the caster, but in most simple weaves it harms you in some way if you violate the seal's directive."

"What directive does this one have?" Ared said.

"I don't know, but you cannot bind someone against their will. He would have to agree to it." Faedra leaned closer to the scroll.

"So the fat scribe is still being untruthful to us."

"Yes, he has to be."

THE CROWN OF SIGHT

"Is there any danger to me?" Darathel said. "Will I be fine, should a break the seal?"

"It is incapable of affecting you," Faedra said.

Darathel nodded, then pushed his thumb against the soft black mass. It broke apart, and Darathel nearly dropped the scroll. Blood was welling up from the paper and began to drip on the floor.

"Goddess of Light," Darathel said, holding the paper at arm's length. He tore his eyes from the strange image at the sound of the scribe falling over. His dark eyes were bulging, and his face had turned beet red.

"What's wrong with him?" Ared said, leaning over the man. "Faedra, can you-" He paused as Faedra gently touched his shoulder.

"There is nothing you can do," Faedra said. "His soul is being torn from his body. Part of the spell of the seal."

Ared shook his head as he tried to roll Yami onto his back. With effort he got the scribe roll over, but life had already left him. He stared into the still, brown eyes for a moment.

"How strange," Darathel said. "He looks like a painting or statue now, not quite like a dead beast."

"It is man's nature," Faedra said. "Be assured that is just a husk. Yami is gone."

"Perhaps he died because we didn't let him deliver it to the king himself," Ared said.

"You were ready to lop his head off," Darathel said.

"Ready, but... Dreamer, this feels wrong." He stood up, still staring at the body. "I feel stupid, but... What do you do with a human husk?"

"Bury it," Faedra said. "Or burn it."

"Ared," Darathel said. "Can you find some guard to help you dispose of this man?"

"I suppose," Ared said. "What was on that scroll, anyway?"

"Oh," Darathel said. He looked down at the scroll, which had stopped bleeding. He spread it open and scanned the neat lines of text. "The king of the Draesenith is challenging my father to single combat. The crown and the kingdom as stakes. He'll leave if my father wins, and take his army with him."

"Why?" Ared said. "He's got our backs to the wall here."

"Most likely his army is tired of being away from home and is getting restless and hungry," Darathel said.

"We'll have to refuse," Faedra said.

"Not necessarily," Darathel said. "Perhaps I could take my father's place."

"He won't permit his son to take such a risk," Faedra said.

"How do we know Katach isn't lying?" Ared said.

"There's another seal on the scroll. A seal that binds Katach," Faedra said, leaning over Darathel's arms to observe the message. "Bound in his own blood. Written by a mystic scribe – the man Yami, I would guess. You cannot forge such a thing."

"But can you violate it?" Ared said. "Can you avoid the magic?"

"Obviously not," Faedra said, gesturing to Yami's body.

"I'll have to take it to the king," Darathel said.

"Surely you aren't taking this seriously enough to bother rousing him," Ared said.

"It is not up to me to determine. This message is for my father," Darathel said. "And despite his labors, he is still the sovereign lord of this realm."

"I want to see him, too," Ared said.

"It has been a long time," Faedra said. "What changes your mind about seeing the lord now?"

"It's not *my* mind you ought to be worried about." He looked at the body on the floor with disgust. "Mardrel will know what to do with this body. I'll send for him and meet you at the king's chamber."

8

Ared, Faedra, and Darathel stepped closer to the desk. Pelanel was bent over, the shining crown pulsing on top of his head. In his hand was a ragged quill. It rushed over the page, words flying from its tip in immaculate forms. Once Pelanel finished the page, the ink vanished, fading to black dust which blew away with the king's ragged breath. The pen moved to the top of the paper, almost of its own accord, skipping past the inkwell that stood forgotten just to Pelanel's right. The writing began anew, so quickly that Darathel could scarcely read the words before the page was once again full. Again, the ink dried to dust and blew away.

"Your Highness," Ared said.

The king looked up, his hand pausing mid-word on the page.

"Ared," he said. "I haven't seen you in ages."

"My apologies. I've been occupied with our defense."

"Yes, the siege that never ends. It has been on my mind," Pelanel said. He looked back at the page and began writing again.

"What are you writing?" Faedra said.

"Our story," Pelanel said. "Or what we have of it so far. I'm changing a few things. Making things as they ought to have been."

Faedra locked eyes with Darathel, her lids and brow drawn down with care.

"Father," Darathel said. "We have received a message from Katach."

"Let me see it," Pelanel said. He reached out and took the scroll suddenly from Darathel's loose hands. His eyes flashed over the words, and he smiled. Immediately, he flipped the paper over and began writing a response.

"It... He wants to fight you one-on-one," Darathel said.

"I can read," Pelanel said. With a flick of his pen, the king scratched his palm. Fresh blood welled up, and he pressed it to the page. With a single stroke Pelanel drew a symbol in crimson and the blood danced, then lay still, shining nearly silver in the light of the crown.

"My lord, no!" Ared said. "You can't accept such a challenge."

"I already have," Pelanel said.

"You can't trust a man like Katach," Ared said.

"Of course not. I trust the magic, though. The magic is real." He stood up quickly and walked to the other side of the room, the light from the hidden windows above suddenly growing enough for them to see the scattered furniture of the bedchamber. "I have my own magic, too." He opened a drawer in a tall dresser and drew forth a sphere the size of a large fruit. It was like a pearl, but its iridescence seemed in flux, shifting and swirling over its surface. He spoke softly to the sphere, and it flashed, leaving in its pattern a strange image of his face, like in negative relief.

"This is one enemy that I would not trust my magic to overcome. Our last sortie reports-"

"He will have to bind himself to this," Pelanel said, holding the sphere up to Ared. "So that each of us will have our own guarantee of honesty." He went back over to the writing table and picked up the scroll. He handed it and the sphere to Ared. "Now excuse me, there is much more to be written."

He sat back down. The quill leapt from the table into his fingers, and Darathel flinched. The words continued from where the king had left off, the ink turning to dust as he returned to the top of the page. The light coming from the windows above dimmed. A halo remained around the crown and the table.

"Yes, very little time," Pelanel said. "This will make it all easier. Much easier on all of you."

Ared stared at the objects in his hands and frowned. His eyes grew brighter, turning from yellow to white.

"You have no right to gamble the crown of Sight Herself," Ared said.

"It is mine to dispense with as I will," Pelanel said calmly, not looking up from his work.

"Wait," Darathel said. "Katach was not merely speaking metaphorically? He wants the literal Crown of Sight?"

"Why else would he ask for crown *and* kingdom?" Faedra said.

"You've spent too much time in the mundane," Ared said. "You are thinking like a human."

"That's what Katach is. Or nearly so. The Draesenith *are* mortals," Darathel said.

"Not quite," Ared said. He looked down on Pelanel. "But more to the point, he has no right to gamble the crown."

"I said it is mine," Pelanel said.

"The crown cannot belong to an individual."

"It is the duty and right of the sovereign to dispense with property, even that owned by the people," Pelanel said.

"It is not due to your people alone. I would lay claim to it."

Pelanel stopped writing and looked up. "You are dispossessed of your title, Ared. You cannot speak for all of the dark elves."

"They have no other representative."

"Nevertheless, you lack the right. And as a matter of fact, so does your race. The crown has never been a possession of those who refused the change. Always it has stayed with the heirs of the Empress of Light. I am the heir." He turned back down and continued his furious writing.

Ared growled and reached slowly, hesitantly toward his sword. A stiff hand from Darathel froze him, keeping him from reaching the hilt of his weapon.

"You shall not countermand my father," he said. "Nor assault him in his chamber."

Pelanel paused. "I wonder if I shall leave this part out, or keep it in for drama." The king sighed. "I shall have to make the decision when I reach that section." The pen began its rapid dance again.

Ared scowled at Darathel. "Do you have any idea what will happen if you allow a man like Katach to possess the Crown of Sight? Have you any thought for the world?"

"If you knew more of the substance of this artifact," Faedra said. "You would not have as much fear. Even if he were to possess it, Katach is mortal-"

Ared scoffed. "You've all spent too long cooped up in your own fixed creations. The warlord at our gates is no mere mortal."

"You worry too much," Pelanel said. "He's no match for me."

"In your present condition-"

"My condition is excellent. I'm stronger than ever."

"Strength is not my concern," Ared said. "How will you maintain this city while focusing on a fight to the death with the most feared warrior in the world-that-is?"

"You doubt my power?" Pelanel said. "Never, Ared, have you-"

"You are avoiding the point, my lord," Ared said, relaxing his shoulders and letting a stiff breath flow between his teeth.

THE CROWN OF SIGHT

"Leave the crown here, my lord," Faedra said. "I will take it up, and maintain the city and the flows of the Prim while you fight Katach. Our mages will still have the magic needed for our people to eat."

"It is already bound," Pelanel said. "Ared, deliver my message to the lord of the Draesenith. Fetch me when it is time for us to end this. You all must leave me now. My concentration wavers, and I have much to do."

"As you wish, my lord," Ared said. "I shall not break my oaths." The dark elf bowed, his eyes cooling to a pale yellow. He turned and walked away from the light as Pelanel began furiously writing once more.

Darathel stared at his father for a protracted time, listening to the steady cadence of the pen scratching the unending, ever-filling page. Amid his father's breaths he heard words he did not understand. He drew his gaze away when he felt Faedra's hand touch his face softly. He turned to look at her, and he saw that she had her hood down, revealing a face that was placidly smooth, but this calmness did not touch her eyes, which were wet and trembling.

He nodded and turned from his father. Faedra wrapped an arm around one of his, then gripped his hand. As they stepped into the darkness, he could feel, more than hear, soft weeping from the high mage. In the echoes between the desk and the curtain of darkness that was Pelanel's door, Darathel allowed himself a moment of release and joined Faedra in a few soft racks and ragged breaths.

9

Ared walked alone to the outward fortifications of the Draesenith army. He carried in one hand a long flag of white. Tucked under the other arm was a leather satchel containing the orb of binding and the contract that had cost a messenger his life, along with a few other items Ared had packed as last resort for an escape. As he neared the camp, he could hear the voices of the enemy echoing in their strange, shifting tongue. He looked up as he approached the main pickets, complete with a make-shift gate of logs fixed together. The ravaged countryside looked like a desert now, and Ared wondered how there were ever enough trees for such a long wall. Logs cut into great spikes pointed at him from two wings thrust forward from the gate. Upon them hung the bodies of men in various states of decay, stripped and empty. Ared wondered if they were intended to be frightening.

"I come bearing a message!" He called out as two grey-skinned warriors leaned out of a wooden merlon and knocked arrows into horn bows. They shouted at each other, but Ared understood none of it.

One held a palm to him, then disappeared from the battlement.

"I'll wait," Ared said. He stuck his flag into the ground. After a minute of waiting, he began pacing around the flag in circles. More eyes had gathered on the ramparts surrounding him. Many, he saw, belonged to men, who were shorter and slighter than their compatriots, but much more fair of face, reflecting, Ared supposed, some descent from the high elves. Their stares all seemed hungry to him; he often had a hard time reading the will of mortals on their faces.

At last, the wooden gate swung upward, revealing a tall and lean draesen, his armor lacquered a deep blue. He walked forward and Ared guessed he was a soldier of some distinction and age, for his face was weathered and wrinkled, and the soldiers all stopped talking as he approached.

"Where is Yami?" he said.

THE CROWN OF SIGHT

"The messenger?" Ared said, looking up into the cold, brown eyes of the draesen. "He died after we read the message. I come bearing the reply."

"Then he betrayed us. Tell me, dark elf, what is the manner of the reply? Yea or nay?"

"I would speak with Katach," Ared replied.

"I would know first, lest his wrath fall on the messenger."

"I cannot say," Ared said. "Except that I require the presence of the king."

"Very well. This way. I am Saren, last general of this army." The draesen turned, flourishing a maroon cloak, and strode toward the open gate. Ared skipped to catch him, leaving the flag planted in the ground.

"I am Ared. I am advisor to king Pelanel."

"He sends valuable servants."

"That is relative," Ared said. "I was greeted by a general."

"Most of my soldiers don't speak High Elven, so don't feel too complimented. You were wise to come unarmed. It gave the humans pause enough to not shoot you and loot your message for themselves."

"The white flag means nothing?"

"Not nothing, but certainly not enough to avoid getting a free kill, and maybe a coin or two from your pockets. We've been through this before, elf. You kill the messenger, and they'll always send another." He stopped. "We will need to check you for secreted arms, before you see the emperor." He nodded to two Draesen, even larger than himself, who stepped forward.

They patted down Ared, checking cuffs and boots for hidden knives. Finding none, they looked in the satchel and, seeing nothing in it that interested them, they handed it back. Ared smiled slightly, knowing that his simple spell had worked; his cache of smoke bombs and cutting implements remained undetected.

The camp beyond the pickets was dense and dirty, filled with tents of a variety of designs, some clearly of different cultural origin than the Draesenith. Females roamed here and there, but none were armed or had the look of mages. Some were elves, some were human. None were of the species of the bulk of the army, so Ared reckoned they were slaves. In the eastern end rose a great mound of dirt and earth. Men and draesen worked at its top, and its appearance gave Ared a feeling of sickening dread.

"Admiring the altar?" Saren said. "Tonight we shall consecrate it. Pray you do not get to admire it up close, while Katach does his duties as priest."

Ared turned his gaze to Saren. "Tell me, last general, who will this army obey if Katach falls?"

"Me, or nobody."

"There is no first general?"

"Be wary of having a loose tongue with Katach," Saren said. "He's been known to cut them out."

"Of course."

"I'm the last general because I am the last alive. Katach does not promote those who are unworthy to the highest post."

"I see."

Ared followed Saren up a hill and through a few pickets to a smaller assemblage of tents. One tall tent stood out from the rest. It was made of cloth like canvas, but dyed an improbable black. A guard stood nearby, straightening up as Saren approached. After a few quick words, Saren stepped past, with Ared following closely. The interior of the tent was lit by lanterns of some magical variety, different than what Ared had seen before.

Near a water basin stood a bare-chested Draesen, running a wet towel over his arms. His large face, heavy-boned, seemed to be in a perpetual dark smile. His long black hair hung loose. He glanced up as Saren approached.

"Lord, here is the messenger from the elves," Saren said. "Yami-"

"Is dead, I know," Katach said. He picked up a dry towel and ran it over his arms as he turned from them and walked past a privacy screen. Glancing around it, Ared saw a young elf maiden reclining in an overlarge bed, holding a sheet up to her chin.

"Get out of here," Katach said to her. "There's imperial business to attend to."

She nodded and, after locking eyes with Ared for a fleeting second, slipped out of the bed, revealing smooth white skin and long dark hair. Ared, despite himself, watched the naked elf slide across the room and gather up her clothes.

"You like her, eh?" Katach said to Ared. "Melala is her name. A noble from the Frostbacks."

"So the northern kingdom has fallen," Ared said.

"It lives on as a province of my empire, of course. I was thinking of making her a wife." He nodded to the elf as she slipped out of a different flap. "I can get you one just like her."

Ared paused. "What?"

"Address me as lord, or something similar," Katach said. "I'm not picky with words, just make the gesture."

"Yes. Your Highness. I didn't understand what you meant."

Katach chuckled. He picked up a shirt and slipped it over his head. "I could use a dark elf for the next campaign. I figure you'll be needing some work once I take the king's head and mop up the city." Katach snapped his fingers. "Is there a female in the city that you have your eye on?"

"No, your Highness, I think not."

Katach looked at Saren. "He's lying. Not a good way to begin a relationship. I hate it when people lie to me."

"What I mean is," Ared said, "that I would not force a maiden-"

"You think like a slave. Interesting, from a dark elf. We'll have to break those bonds if you want to be successful under my command. Now, to business. What does the king answer me, if he saw my message?"

"He saw it."

"After Yami died."

"Yes, but lord-"

"Well, what is it? Shall I cut off his head in front of the city, or after I have sacked it?"

Ared shook his head. "I came myself so that I could entreat with you. Apart from the king."

"Oh? You have something to bargain with me? Saren, fetch a pen."

"Aye, sire," Saren said, and went over to a nearby desk.

"What can I do to persuade you not to engage the king in combat?" Ared said.

"You have to offer me something," Katach said. "That's how this works. Otherwise you aren't entreating, you are begging."

"How about your life?" Ared said.

"Are you threatening me?" Katach said. He snapped his fingers and Ared doubled over in pain, his insides writhing. "That's a taste."

The pain stopped, and Ared gasped. "No," he said with effort. He thought briefly of his knives in his satchel, but knew there was no way he could put them to use against the emperor. He seemed to radiate power. At the same time, Ared felt certain Pelanel could not overcome the draesen. "Not a threat. A warning. You do not know the nature of the city you assault."

"Stone, mortar, wood. All these things I have razed before."

"Not quite," Ared said, struggling to his feet. "The city is a high-elf creation."

"I have several elven cities under my heel. I have died at none of them."

"Those cities were built. This one was created. Without the master, it will decay. Quickly."

Katach shook his head. "Foolishness. The power that binds the realm of Pelanel is not his own. He is not essential to it, nor to its working." He saw Ared's eyes brighten for a moment, and he opened his mouth in a smile, revealing sharp teeth. "Yes, dark elf, I know of the Crown that once belonged to the Goddess of Sight. Why else would I concern myself with your tiny, insignificant realm?"

Ared took a breath. "I see. Here is the response from the king." He reached into his satchel and withdrew both the orb and the contract. He handed them to Katach. "It's called a binding orb. It will prevent you from breaking faith."

"Prevent me, eh? I see the king signed my contract. Let *him* try getting out of *that*."

"He will not break it. He is stubborn, and unafraid of you."

"He doesn't know me yet," Katach said. "It is good he agreed, though. This will save much bloodshed and suffering for your people."

"Is that something you care about?" Ared said.

"Watch your tongue," Saren said from where he sat, writing.

Katach smiled. "If I didn't, I know that *you* do. And I need my soldiers in good a state if I will be taking them into the fractured realms. You see why I offer a good employment opportunity now, yes?"

"You think I would betray my people?"

Katach laughed. "Why would I think that, general?"

Saren looked up. "You're not with *your* people. That means you're either a vagabond and hate your own people, or you are an outcast and they hate you. Your knowledge would be valuable, Ared. The rewards are great, if you serve well."

"Listen to your betters, elf," Katach said. "I will bind myself to this orb as your king requests. I fear him not." The ball sprang to light in Katach's hand, the surface swirling before taking on the dusty image of the warlord. He tossed it to Ared, who caught it. It felt heavier than before. "Take that back to your king as proof of my honesty. Then, return to me."

"I will take this to the king," Ared said.

Katach smiled and looked at Saren. "He's clever with those words. Escort him out."

Saren nodded and stood up. Ared followed him out of the tent and back toward the gate.

"It was wise to stop trying to treat with Katach," Saren said. "He doesn't change course once he has set it."

"Indeed, I can see that."

"His offer is limited, so you know."

"I cannot break an oath of fealty," Ared said.

"Then see me after your master has been slain, though you will lose what you could gain by switching sides now."

10

"You may enter, my prince."

Darathel paused at the sound of Faedra's voice, then pushed open the door to her chamber. The doors to the balcony were open, letting it the late afternoon light. The curtains waved in the breeze, and Darathel caught sight of the high mage between their movements. She stood against a stone rail on the balcony, gazing west, toward the Fay Lands. The sun caught her pale skin and lit it evenly, an expanse of snow punctuated by eyes that burned blue. Her cloak was gone, and she wore a simple dress of pale blue silk that revealed her small, almost delicate, frame.

"How did you know it was me?" Darathel said, pushing aside a curtain and exiting out to the balcony.

"You tripped one of my wards."

"You've been setting wards?"

"Yes." She turned east, and the sun lit up her golden head. A single hair was out of place in the blonde sheet, and Darathel found himself watching it move in the wind. "The enemy is close. The castle could be infiltrated."

"You don't dress as if you are so concerned."

"It's good to take a step away, while we still can."

"If you had doubts about the security, I could have-"

"Not necessary, Darathel. The security is as good as it can be. I'm just cautious. Or paranoid, maybe. They have built something that disturbs me."

"What is it?" Darathel said, moving beside Faedra and looking out over the wards of the castle, the winding city streets, and to the fields beyond, where a reek went up from the enemy camp.

"I can't see it, but I can feel it is something bad. Something wicked. My gift of forbearance..." She looked at Darathel, her face placid save for a stitch mid-brow. "I am blind."

"It is a fickle gift, I hear."

"At the best of times, but it has kept us ahead thus far."

"What blinds you?"

"Something more powerful than me." She sighed. "But I worry only about myself, when I should worry about you."

"What is there to worry about with me?"

"Your father," Faedra said. "Surely what you saw disturbed you."

Darathel nodded. "I would be lying if I said it did not, but I did not feel wholly unsure about things until I saw you cry."

"I'm sorry for that."

"I always trusted the matters of the Eternal Dream to my father and to you. The moment you began crying I knew the trance was not a normal thing. What do you think he was doing?"

"It was some sort of magic, though I know not where he learned it. It seemed like he was trying to write a story. The history of this city." Faedra moved closer to Darathel, then leaned against him, putting her head on his chest. He wrapped his arms lightly about her. "I think he knows the city will fall. That's why he is in a hurry. He wants to impart this place some kind of permanency within and beyond the world that is."

"Why would he agree to the fight?"

"I don't know. He is of two minds – one a desperate lord facing death, the other a respected hero who founded a kingdom."

"What do I do?"

"There is little you can do, except plan for the fall, and hope his foresight is clouded like mine. Or hope that the hero is right." She took a deep breath. "Suddenly I am filled with regret."

"I am too." He glanced west, to the Fay Lands, which appeared as an ever-stretching forest, wreathed in mist. "I have never told you how much I care for you."

Faedra looked up at him and smiled, tears in the corners of her eyes. She reached a hand up and touched his smooth face. "I remember you when you were a little boy. There are so many things that are the same in your face. Though I loved you then, now..." She frowned. "I hold two images in my mind: one the fleeting youth I loved like a brother, the other the proud prince I have come to admire as my equal."

THE CROWN OF SIGHT

"But do you still love me?"

"As a boy, and as a prince. I shall love you as a king, too."

"I won't have a kingdom."

"I'll follow you anyway."

Darathel smiled. "Even into the heart of the Fay?"

She smiled again. "Yes. I'll follow you. Why have you never revealed your heart to me?"

"I could ask you the same question."

"The answer might be the same," Faedra said. "There are other matters besides love. But you have the liberty to speak, not me."

"I don't know, then." Darathel frowned. He looked again to the Fay Lands, his vision drawn there almost against his will. The sun was setting behind the hills, and amid the swirling fog, the forest within grew sharper in detail. Light was growing from inside it.

"You felt it, too?" Faedra said. "Of course you did. You have the spark, after all."

"I do?"

"Of course. I've always wanted to refine your spell-working."

Darathel rubbed his head. "What was that feeling?"

"Something is stirring within the Fay Lands," Faedra said. She smiled in earnest. The wind picked up and began to bite their eyes, causing them both to tear up and squint. "Something good. I felt right, for a moment."

"Me too," Darathel said. "It is the first right feeling in a long time, actually."

"Where is Ared?"

"He left through the secret entrance on a scouting expedition, why?"

"He is in danger."

11

Katach stepped toward the altar, his black cloak billowing in the wind, revealing glances of his garb of crimson and midnight. Made of earth and wood, the altar was simpler than the one in Dagolara. That one, the cap of the Infinite Ziggurat which was itself the center of the capital, was made of gold, and Katach had added to it with his many conquests, not so much an offering as an expression of thanks to the greatest god, the dragon Diorgesh. Upon that great altar many sacrifices had been made, the blood made to run down great spouts, over seraphs with dragon wings, and collected into golden basins, where the elite could share in the leavings and enter temporary communion with Diorgesh the Unbinder.

The altar in the war camp, though not yet dedicated to the greatest god, would nonetheless be recognized by him. Katach shared a deep communion with his god, the whisperings of the dragon's unfathomable mind tickling him frequently, especially at sunset. Even so close to the Fay, the chaos Diorgesh despised, his bond remained. As the lord of the Draesenith watched the sun redden behind the white city, he could feel the mind of the Unbinder, and knew he would accept the sacrifice and hear his request. More than that, he knew his request would be granted, for it furthered the aims of mighty Diorgesh.

Katach tossed his cloak back. His loose pants and shirt, made of black silk, caught the rays of the dying sun and shimmered. His belt of red leather, bound by a buckle of pure gold, shined brightly. On his chest was the sigil of the high priest, for as Emperor he was all at once king, consul, and clergy.

"Let the Unbinder hear my voice, and accept this sacrifice," he said, his voice magically amplified. "Let him roll back the primal chaos, and unbind us from the tyranny of destiny."

THE CROWN OF SIGHT

He glanced down from the earthen mound and nodded. Two priests at the bottom caught his gesture and ascended, carrying between them a naked female elf that struggled vainly against their grip. They brought her to the edge of the wooden platform, and held her before Katach.

"Melala," the emperor said. He looked down at her body, taking in the details, then at her face, which was contorted in fear and weeping. Her beautiful hair was tangled. Katach's eyes darkened slightly. "Never have I known a creature as beautiful as you. Even my first wife, jealous as she is, would admit the same. You would have been mother to kings of the strongest line, priests of Diorgesh."

The elf said nothing. Katach forced a smile. He knew Diorgesh wanted a sacrifice to be meaningful. Something must be lost.

He turned to his left, where another priest stood by. She held forth a long dagger of hardened gold and dark steel, her eyes downcast.

"Do you fear to look upon your god's favored?"

"Yes," she said.

"It is well." He took the dagger. The elf struggled anew. He reached forward and gripped her head.

"I'll return," she said raggedly. "Pray it is long after you are dead, mortal."

Katach laughed softly. "Mortal, eh? You are powerless now, and so you shall be if you return. But no, I think there will be no returning from Diorgesh."

Before she could answer him, he slit her throat. He made four more quick cuts to her wrists and inner thighs. He then threw her onto the wooden platform, and watched her writhe for a few protracted moments, then lay still, her eyes closed but twitching. Quietly the priest to his left handed him a golden goblet. He took it and knelt down. In a makeshift basin below the elf was a collection of blood, nearly black in the fading light.

Katach dipped the goblet in, filling it to the brim, and drained it. Immediately he felt the presence of his god, infusing his body, giving him strength. He also felt the receding of the Prim, its chaotic power, which he could draw upon when communion grew weak, giving way to the paths of Diorgesh, unbinding the many things from the magic of creation that would normally have a hold on him. The magic of the Prim, so immutable in its essence, became meaningless. His mind sharpened, and he smiled a red-lipped smile.

He dipped the cup in again and stood up. He handed it to the priest on his left. Humbly, she bowed and took the cup. She drank from it, then handed it to the other two priests.

"Saren, come forth and join us," Katach said. He nodded to the last priest, who knelt down to fill the goblet again.

The general, wearing still his armor, began to trudge up the earthen embankment. Before he reached the top, the assembled priests and soldiers gave a collected cry of surprise.

On the alter, the elf's body had burst into violet flames, sending sparks flying into the dusk. Saren hurried up, shielding his eyes from the light and heat. Katach drew his cloak about himself, trying to block a sudden pain on his skin. The elf's body was disappearing, radiating out fire of a multitude of colors from a core of white light in the center of her being. Katach looked down and saw that the blood, too, was on fire. The priest who had knelt to fill the goblet was dead, charred beyond recognition.

Katach touched his chest, wondering if the blood would ignite within him and burn him from the inside out. He felt only the warmth of it, along with the presence of his god.

On the wooden altar, the flames receded. The body was gone, leaving no trace of its existence, but the platform was still on fire. Mundane orange flames licked the toes of those surrounding it. The body of the fallen priest continued to burn as if on a pyre.

"Sire, should we save his body?" Saren said.

"We lack the means," Katach said.

"I can pull it out with a stout spear."

"And let his soul return to a charred wreck? No, his spirit will wander. It is unfortunate for a high priest, but unavoidable." He turned to his left. The priest there was visibly trembling. "I take it you have never seen something like this before?"

"No, lord," she said.

"Well, Faress, you are the second high priest now."

"What happened?"

"Someone stole our sacrifice," Katach said, scowling. "Some god has freed her and sent her back to the origin."

"Is such a thing possible?"

"Clearly, it is. Only a god would have the power to remove the blood sacrifice. Nonetheless, Diorgesh has heard us. Do you feel him?"

The priest hesitated. "Yes. A little more than before."

Katach turned from the fire and looked to the city. Dusk was deepening to pure night, but the Fay Lands beyond Pelanalda did not obey the turnings of nature. They were aglow, a forest with pale yellow fog swirling behind the city walls, shifting and unknowable.

12

Ared slid through a gap in the pickets where one of the sharpened logs had fallen into a watery mud hole. He held his breath and said a quiet word, feeling the Prim flow through him at the thought and form a barrier, invisible, beyond him. He turned back and nodded. Up through the mud scrambled his two finest assassins: Tara and Talel. They reached him and squatted down behind a pile of building debris, removing their wrapped swords and crossbows from their backs. As they belted their blades on, Ared knelt down to the wet dirt. He drew a quick set of circles.

"We're here. Not where I thought we'd get in, but we are in and though you can't see it, we are very close. The high pavilion is up here. We won't get through there, but you should see it to our left at all times." He heard footsteps and paused, touching his lips with his finger.

Two Draesen walked by, talking in their guttural language. Tara startled slightly as one of them seemed to look at her, but a touch from Ared stilled her, stopping her from drawing her sword.

"That was close," Talel said once he was sure the enemies were out of earshot.

"Closer than you realize," Ared said. "Any closer and the cloaking spell would have failed."

"We would have been able to dispatch them quietly," Tara said.

"Not so quietly that we wouldn't be noticed," Ared said. "Anyway, be extra careful once we leave these wards. You know a few spells that will affect the minds of the enemy, but none of them can make us wholly invisible as we move." He pointed back down at the circles and drew a square. "Here's the altar. That'll be our opportunity, as he won't have his armor on. We'll all fire at once, if possible."

"If we miss?" Talel said. He scratched his chin.

Ared shrugged. "Don't miss. I'll set cloaking wards when we get there, but beware – a fair number of these grey skins have the gift, and they can counter you before you realize it. Keep your distance and stay hidden. Now that we're here, I'm going to go north, round the pavilion. Tara will come with me until we can split off. Talel, you'll go round the south side. If any of us are late, assume we've been caught."

"Aye, sir," Talel said. He moved to the edge of the woodpile. "May the gods guide you."

Ared nodded slowly. "Let's go. If I don't see you again, know that I am thankful for you. Your king's life rests on us."

Talel nodded back and moved out, through the hazy barrier of the ward and into the dusty outskirts of the Draesenith tent city, sticking to the lengthening shadows, using what magic he had learned from Ared to make himself inconspicuous.

"After you, sir," Tara said. Her long hair was tied back and stuffed into her shirt, which was made to look like the simple gambesons some of the humans in the army wore. At a glance, she looked like an adolescent boy, until you caught sight of her ears, tucked as they were into a cloth wrapped around her head.

Ared forced a smile, then moved through the shimmering edges of his spell, Tara moving silently behind him. He breathed out another word, feeling the Prim flow through his teeth like liquid light, and a familiar feeling touched his neck, just out of reach. Nearly soundless, they moved along a line of fortifications, the Draesen milling about seeming to take no notice of them. Whenever the elves approached a guard, something would catch the enemy's eye, or he would become suddenly aware of the fit of his armor, and adjust himself.

Feeling an impulse to change direction, Ared turned into one of the lines of tents, thankful to see it mostly abandoned. Only a lone cook stood in the clearing, fretting over a noxious stew in a great black pot over an open fire. Ared flicked a finger out, and the cook turned around, looking for something, confused that it wasn't there. Tara followed Ared right past the pot and into a narrow stretch of dirt between two long rows of tents.

Working quickly north and then east, they came to a separation in the camp. Pickets held two opposing wards where many draesen and men went down a makeshift avenue. Ared and Tara moved forward and hid against the side of a tent behind a few unused logs.

"Here is where we must part," Ared said. "Follow that line west, and you should reach the altar. I'll take the harder road around the pavilion."

"It's been an honor, sir."

"All mine."

"If I don't make it back…" Tara paused and licked her lips. "There's a treasure I hid behind the statue of Atalthal, in the grand gallery, in a nook under a cracked tile."

"I'll send it off," Ared said. "I have nothing to request. You've been the best."

He put his arm forward and she clasped it, then pulled him into a hug.

"See you soon," Tara said, then released him and, setting a cloaking ward, strode across the path and into a cluster of tents.

Ared knelt down and calmed himself. He breathed out slowly, letting his mind find the spell he wanted in its familiar paths. He watched for a passing group of soldiers, then said a shallow word. The air shimmered for a moment, and he slipped across the path and up an earthen ramp, to the stacked logs and debris that made up the upper pavilion's defenses. Staying just below the wooden ramparts, he stepped lightly on mud and wet turf, working his way around the outside, praying to Verbus, the god of fate and time, that his spell would keep any errant eyes from finding him.

He saw no signs of Draesen or man, and soon realized why when he saw the altar rising above the tents on the south side of the camp. It seemed larger and more imposing than when he had spied it from within the camp the day previous. Around it

THE CROWN OF SIGHT

stood a wide array of soldiers, though nowhere near the entire army. Dusk was coming on quickly, and it calmed Ared. He slid down from the battlement and into a stable area, resting behind a withering pile of straw. The horses meandering about in a makeshift pasture (long bereft of grass) payed him no mind.

He could feel fate at work in a way he had not in a very long time. It was almost as if he was living twice, each footstep anticipated and familiar. He edged along to a fence of stacked scrap wood, made hastily but easy to hide behind, and half-crawled to where he knew he would be able to fire on the emperor. He felt good, suddenly self-assure that he had made the right choice, though it would have gone against the wishes of the king. A slight shimmer ahead let him know that at least one of his subordinates had made it to the fire point.

He checked his surroundings and slipped along the edge of the fence again, glancing off to his right, were a makeshift battlement terminated in a sheer drop to the ruined plain below. A few soldiers stood idle there, but didn't seem interested in what was happening at the altar. He felt himself step across the ward, and suddenly Tara was there, her crossbow in her hand, already loaded.

He smiled at her and unslung his own crossbow. He fit his boot into the stirrup and with a heave spanned it. He settled into a kneel and fitted a poison bolt.

"I dared not get closer," Tara whispered.

"Talel?" Ared said.

Tara shook her head.

Ared's smile slackened. He nodded back. Sliding closer to her he pointed out the emperor: a figure robed in black at the pinnacle of the dirt mound, standing a head taller than the similarly dressed priests around him. He was on the other side of whatever ringed the hill, and only the top half of him was visible.

"Wait for a full presentation," Ared said.

Tara knelt beside him and shouldered her crossbow, using a piece of scrap wood to steady the foregrip against the earth. They waited, watching carefully. A naked elf was brought up, and Tara backed away from her sight for a moment.

"What is that?" she said.

"Quiet. Concentrate," Ared said. He watched as Katach moved slightly, showing more of himself. "On three."

Before he could count, he found his own peace shaken as the elf's blood was spilled and she was thrown forward. The feeling of retreading his steps disappeared, and he felt suddenly confused.

Shouting from nearby brought him out of the haze, and he realized that they were exposed. A group of soldiers was running toward them.

"Now!" Ared shouted. He fired his crossbow, but his heart sank as he watched the bolt fly out at an odd angle, spiraling wildly as it fractured and one of the fletchings fell away. He looked to his left to see shock on Tara's face. A bolt protruded from just below her collarbone. He dropped his crossbow and threw his arms around her. Her own weapon hit the ground with a thud, discharging into the dirt.

He mustered his strength and heaved her up, running for the battlement. It was a long way down, but he might make it, if he could bring forth a current of air to slow them, or... his mind was clouded again as he felt a pain in his hamstring. He knew it was an arrow, and though it bit deeply, he ignored it and kept his pace, shuffling to keep his feet under him and Tara on his shoulders.

He turned back to see two Draesen nearly upon him, both wielding long spears. He spoke a word and threw his hand out, intending to push them back with a conjuring of flame, but nothing happened. Desperate, he tried again, stumbling backwards. Again, nothing happened. His access to the Prim was, he realized, completely severed. His jumbled mind could barely process the problem.

One of the soldiers fell suddenly, a bolt having struck him in the neck. Ared looked to his left to see Talel, dashing toward him with his sword drawn, his crossbow abandoned in the dust.

"Go!" the elf cried. It was his last word. An arrow from somewhere unseen struck him in the back, and he fell, then was quickly pierced by spears as the Draesen rushed him.

Ared felt the tip of a spear hit his side, but out of instinct he spun and it turned out of his flesh, leaving only a shallow wound. Tara felt heavy on his left shoulder and back. In an instant he had his sword drawn. He stepped forward, feeling the shaft of his enemy's weapon slide and sting his ribs, then smashed down with his blade, striking the Draesen's coif just below his helm. It staggered the grey-skinned warrior, and he stumbled backward and fell.

Ared, feeling renewed desperation, ran again toward the battlement, still empty, knowing with a full mind that he could not survive the fall. Where his access to the Prim had gone, he did not know, but he thought vainly that he might at least save Tara, who still breathed, folded over his shoulder. He reached the parapet, made of cut logs and quickly mixed mortar, and looked over the edge. It was a staggering drop to the rocky floor below, but there were a few small oaks perched among the rocks of the cliff that might slow him.

He felt an arrow hit him in the back. His breath left him, and his knees began to give way. He looked back and saw, bright against the east dusk, a tower of flame atop the altar. The flames, bright as the sun, stunned him, and he tore his eyes away. He leaned over the edge and fell with Tara. As his feet left ground a sudden feeling suffused him, and he felt the Prim return. At the same time, he struck one of the trees. His mind returned to its normal clear detachment. He looked down to see the ground, slowly approaching as if time had halted its relentless forward march and given him an armistice, however brief. He also felt his wounds. He looked down to see both light and blood leaking from his leg.

He would die, at long last. Nothing could save him, but as he accepted his fate, he knew also that he yet remained living for a reason. Breathing his last breath, he said a word. The light of the Prim ran through him, and a great wind struck him, blowing his hair back and drying his eyes. The approach to the earth slowed even as time renewed its attack on his failing body.

"Take me, Dreamer," he said in his mind. He felt the first light, like fire, taking his body away from the mundane human world, and he shifted away from consciousness.

13

"What is it? I need no more interruptions!"

Pelanel was hunched over the writing desk, his right hand contorted in pain. His normally serene face glistened with sweat. His brow and eyes, usually lineless, were wrinkled like he was a mortal.

Faedra stepped into the light, her hood down. Light from the windows high above seemed to grow to meet her steps. Darathel stood close behind her.

"What is troubling you, your highness?" Faedra said in a calm monotone.

"You. You are troubling me!" he said, then growled as he forced his hand to commit more ink to the page. The inkwell on the stand nearby was nearly dry, and stray blots stained the wood surface of the desk. "Infernal, bothersome, meddling… Ah!" He grabbed his right hand with his left and began to press into the flesh between his thumb and index finger. "It was all so clear, and then I forgot it. Why! How? Quiet! You're going to make me lose my place!"

"Father," Darathel said, his voice barely above a whisper.

"Go!" Pelanel said. "Get out of here. I have so little time left. I must concentrate!"

"It is time, father," Darathel said. "It is time to don your armor and fulfill your oath to Katach."

"What are you talking about?" Pelanel said. His frowned deepened, then his face suddenly relaxed. "Yes. The fight. I remember now. Is it time already? I must finish this. I must, while I can still remember... but I can't!"

"Unless you want the gates to fall and our walls to fail, we must begin," Darathel said. "I have brought your armor. I will be your squire today."

Pelanel shook his head. He set himself back to the paper, but was stilled by the hand of Faedra, who gently cradled his writing hand in hers, picked it up and helped him place the pen back on its stand.

"But I haven't finished!"

"The time for endings is now, your highness. Your story will have to be written in actions today," Faedra said.

Pelanel took a breath and looked up at Faedra. His face calmed, and his shakes began to subside. Slowly, he reached up and touched her face. "Faedra. Ever faithful have you been to my house." He looked down at the half-filled paper. The words began to fade to grey. "I should have betrothed Darathel to you long ago. Forgive my hesitation. I never should have entertained, even in my mind, anyone but you." He smiled at her.

"You are forgiven."

"Foolish," Pelanel said. "Foolish I have been... to consider politics." He stood up slowly. "I should have changed it. I tried, you see-"

"You still can," Darathel said.

"Right," Pelanel said. He clapped his son on the shoulder. He straightened his back. "I'll see to it after the duel."

"Are you still confident?"

"Of course." Pelanel smiled. "I have slain a dragon. What is a mortal to me?"

"I will help you with your armor," Darathel said. The windows above were now full of light, and the prince motioned to a table where an ancient jack and armor set was neatly stacked.

"Thank you," Pelanel said, stepping toward the armor.

"Your crown," Faedra said. "You should pass it off to either myself or Darathel."

Pelanel narrowed his eyes and reached for the circlet atop his head, which grew to a blinding white. "What? My crown?"

Faedra cast a quick glance to Darathel.

"You cannot wear it with your helm," the prince said. "It will be safe here."

Pelanel shook his head. "Without it, the realm will lose itself."

"Myself or Faedra can wear it," Darathel said. "This place is our home, too. Who knows it better than either of us?"

The crown faded, and Pelanel took a step backward. "You might change things. *Your* mind is not *my* mind."

"Changes are easily remedied," Faedra said. "Besides, what about your book?"

Pelanel gazed at her silently for a long moment. "You are right. I foresaw this, did I not? Yes, but it's permanence is not total. Not yet, with so many pages blank." He looked at his son. "You can wear the crown, my son. You are the next heir to the Empress of Light, after all."

"I would trust Faedra to wear it," Darathel. "But I will accept it."

Slowly, and with almost painful hesitation, Pelanel took the crown from where it sat upon his brow. His face suddenly lightened as he held it in front of himself. The crown lost its bright shine and faded to a golden luster, giving off only a slight amount of its own light. He reached forward and placed it on Darathel's head.

"It looks proper," he said. He looked at Faedra. "You will stay here with him, yes?"

"I will," Faedra said.

Pelanel nodded and stepped to where his armor sat in a pile. He picked up the helm and smiled as he looked upon it. It was a bright, silvery white, but the engraved details had lines of tarnish on them. Carvings of vines and dragons crawled along the brow, above the nose guard, and around the wide skirt that guarded his neck. He put it back down and picked up his curved longsword, which sat oiled in a sheath of leather from a dreadtusk, an ancient and fearsome beast. He took it out a finger and checked its edge.

"My old sword," he said, his eyes waxing. "You have kept it well."

"I have the one mother gave you." Darathel patted the hilt of the sword at his hip.

"She gave it to you, not me, you'll recall." Pelanel pushed the sword back into its sheath. "My soul burns with the memory of these things," the king said. "Katach has signed himself over to the ruin of a destiny far beyond him."

"May it be so," Faedra said, and nodded.

14

The doors swung open, the portcullises were raised, and Pelanel slowly rode forward. The marble statues and fountains of the First Square left his sight and his mind; the hanging vines and eternal blooms were pushed aside to make room for the presence of his war mind, ancient and deadly. Passing into the stone arch, bright and immaculate, he smiled. He admired the handiwork of the front doors, shod by true steel and blessed with the light of the Prim. He could almost see the lines of magic that infused them, making them impenetrable.

He took a breath, feeling more at ease than he had felt in a long time, though he marched out to engage in mortal combat. His mind was clear and simple again, no longer burdened with the unending task of renewing his creation, perched perilously on the edge of the Fay, and the brutal exercise of channeling the Prim for use by the city mages. The field before him was empty and barren. He chanced one last glance over his shoulder, and spied his son and Faedra far away, on the second battlement, their figures small and lonely.

He nudged his horse forward, onto the drawbridge. The clap of hooves on the eternal wood rang out loudly over the moat, now more mud than water. The dirt on the field, once filled with rich grass, turned to billowing dust as his horse trotted to the appointed place. The armies of the Draesenith, vast and dark, were arrayed in front of the palisades of their camp, ranked and filed as if preparing for battle. Perhaps they feared some deception on his part at the end. Among the lines the king spotted his enemy, tall and imposing in armor of lacquered black.

The wind shifted to Pelanel's back as he dismounted. He slapped his horse lightly on the rump, and it trotted away, back toward the city, which he saw had already closed itself back up. The horse would wait patiently for him, as it had for many centuries.

"Here I am, Katach!" Pelanel shouted over the wind. "Come and fulfill your oath! Say whatever prayers you wish to your gods!"

THE CROWN OF SIGHT

"Fool." It was a cold, calm voice. It rang in Pelanel's ears as if spoken by someone beside him. Distant, Katach raised his arm.

Pelanel had a fraction of a second to react. He shielded his face as he saw a hail of arrows flying toward him. He felt the impact on his armor. Ancient was that suit, made by smiths who forged with magic rather than fire in the age when the sun was dead, but for all its history and glory, the resiliency of the plates and mail failed. Darts parted links and burrowed into Pelanel's flesh. He felt the sting of dozens of them on his hands, chest, legs, and arms.

Pelanel reached in his mind for his memories of the Prim. Magic surged through him, and his first thought, simple and chaotic, was of fire. His flesh burned as the arrows ignited, falling from his armor and skin in an instant. He lowered his hand and drew his sword. Katach was far away. Ignoring his pain, the king rushed toward the emperor.

"Your betrayal will be your doom!" he shouted hoarsely.

"There is nothing that can bind me," Katach whispered back, clear as crystal.

Another hail of arrows descended upon the king of the Bastion Elves, the last great lord of the High Elves in the world-that-is, and he fell to the ground, pierced in a dozen places. He reached again for fire, his anger burning through his surprise, but found it weak and unwilling.

Still, his life was yet in his veins and he stood up and pushed forward. Waves of magic assaulted him, kicking up dust and charring dead grass. He walked through it, feeling his flesh peel and wither. His armor was hanging by threads and straps, and his legs were heavy. He reached again for the magic that was familiar to him, but he was confused. He could no longer remember the concepts he sought. He could not remember words to help him. He forgot where he was and why he was there, or what was supposed to happen next.

He fell to his knees, then his eyes swam. A fresh wave of magic, flung from every direction, struck him, and he was gone.

15

Darathel felt Faedra's arms under his as his sight blurred. His knees felt numb, and he realized that what he had just seen – just felt – was real. He put a hand against one of the merlons to steady himself, allowing his telescope to roll away on the floor. Faedra's grip on him relaxed. The Crown of Sight felt suddenly heavy and dull.

"He broke the oath," Faedra said. "Why would he-"

She could not finish giving voice to her thought. A great rumble shook them, and they both fell to their knees, their ears nearly ringing in the din. Darathel pushed himself and Faedra back up. Over the battlement they could see dust rising from the buildings in the city. The great gate, which had stood for months against the onslaught of the Draesenith hordes, was swaying and rippling, like a reflection in a pond. With a cacophonous crash, the entire structure collapsed: drawbridge, doors, portcullis, archway, turrets… everything fell to the ground. As the dust began to blow on the breeze, Darathel realized that dust was all that was left; the gate left no ruble or ruin. It was simply gone.

The walls on either side, the impenetrable first defense of the city, began to rumble and crumble as well, taking soldiers and defensive trebuchets with them.

Darathel took a breath and said. "What is happening? Is the crown failing to preserve the city?"

"No. The magic of the oathstone is undoing our defenses," Faedra said. "It is holding your father to his oath. The city is forfeit. Katach has devised some way to break the binding of the oathstone and his contract, but it has not unbound the king."

"How is that possible?"

"I don't know, but this is unmistakable. If he had this power all along he would have used it earlier. If it was the crown... things would not fall. Not like this."

They both fell down at another crash. Darathel looked away and saw dust rising from the second gate. Back across the field, the army of the Draesenith was advancing.

"Quickly, we need to get off of this wall," he said. "We'll gather who we can and make a stand at the keep." Darathel stood up and grabbed Faedra's hand. He pulled her toward the stair, and then hesitantly descended, leaning on the rumbling wall for support.

"I don't think that will work," Faedra said.

"It's all we have. I owe a duty to preserve the city if I can."

"I will follow you, but do not hold to hope. We ought to begin the evacuation to the Fay Lands."

"The people aren't prepared," Darathel said. They reached the street and saw the chaotic moving of the city-dwellers, obscured by a choking cloud of dust. "Ared has disappeared, and we have nobody to guide the people."

"All the same," Faedra said. "That is their best chance at survival."

Darathel watched the chaos for a long moment, then said, "You're right." He charged through the dust to a group of bewildered soldiers shouting at each other. "You there! Spread word, quickly. Every maid, matron, and child is to go to the gates west of the keep and flee into the Fay. Everyone with the spark or able to bear arms is to assemble at the castle, whether the gate stands there or not."

The soldiers saluted and dispersed, still hesitant with confusion.

"We can delay them a little, at least," Darathel said.

16

Katach toed the ashes and burnt armor of what was once Pelanel, the high-elven king. The links were parted and rusted, turned to dust in places, and the various plates were tarnished and dull. The remnants of the jack fell away as the emperor knelt down to look inside the empty, shattered helm.

"The gatehouse has collapsed on itself," Saren said from atop his horse. "It looks like your plan worked."

Katach tossed the helm away and mounted his horse. "Not exactly. The king was not so foolish as to wear the Crown of Lady Sight. I want nobody to loot until we have seized the city and the crown itself. Now we will test the discipline of your command."

"Understood, sir. Do you think they will still be able to resist?"

"The soldiers were not bound as their king was. Expect a fight."

"Without their defenses, they will be easily crushed."

"They still have magic at their disposal, and their backs are to the wall. Do not take these elves lightly, Saren."

"I will have my warriors exercise the appropriate caution, and I will integrate our own mages. With the blessing of Diorgesh, their magic will be of no offensive use."

"The blessing was stolen, but do as you suggest anyway." Katach nodded. "I will lead our elites."

"Yes, sir."

THE CROWN OF SIGHT

17

"Sire."

Darathel turned at the breathy voice, and the commanders went silent. Around the corner of the fallen gate, the last great line of defense before the keep, came Tara, one of Ared's trusted agents. She limped slowly, her face dirty. Blood oozed from a wound in her chest that her hand held taut. She was dressed in the armor of a Draesen, though it fit her poorly.

One of the captains rushed over to hold her up.

"What happened?" Darathel said.

Faedra pushed her hood back and leaned close. "I will attempt to heal it, but I will need some time."

"Don't worry about me," Tara said, pushing back Faedra. "I made it this far. I'm only tired. I won't fade just yet."

"I intend to make sure you won't," Faedra said.

"I'm too late, but-" Tara winced as Faedra touched the wound. "But I must report, lord." She fell to her knees.

"Where is Ared?" Darathel said, kneeling beside her.

"Departed. We infiltrated the camp, with the intent of assassinating Katach."

Darathel gritted his teeth. "Ared *would* try something like that."

"We would have been successful, but something happened. All our magic was stolen away from us, and we were exposed. Talel is gone, too, I think. They killed an elvish maiden. Sacrificed her to…" Tara shook her head, as if confused. "Diorgesh." She closed her eyes.

"Diorgesh," Faedra said. She gazed off into space. "That explains it. I never would have thought… but then, they *are* mortals."

"What is it?" Darathel said.

Faedra snapped her head back to one of the captains. "Get Tara to somewhere where she can rest. The healing will take a bit of time, but she should be fit to flee soon." The captain nodded and picked up Tara in his arms. He handed her off to another soldier.

"Diorgesh is a dragon, yes?" Darathel said. "One of the old aspects."

"Yes. The Unbinder. Katach must have some sort of connection with him. Which explains why he could violate the oaths. Diorgesh is opposed to the Fay and all its magic. As a dragon he is a contradiction in terms, but he somehow exists and is apparently still at work in the world."

"Then the Fay really is the safest place," Darathel said. "I never thought that would end up being the case."

"I never thought the greatest liar would be worshipped as a god," Faedra said. "These mortals are mad!"

18

The Draesenith warriors were strong beyond anything Darathel had reckoned was possible. He had seen only short skirmishes from cover, where it was easy to hit hard and escape to the marches around the city, where the mist coming from the Fay Lands lay thick and confused the grey-skinned giants. The sorties during the siege had not prepared him for the reality of a hard battle with no retreat. His soldiers were being slaughtered, line after line. The ward between the outer castle wall and the keep, both missing their gates, was too small to maneuver, but also too narrow for the attackers to get through to the last portals of escape. The elven mages, even so close to the Fay, were unable to bring the destruction of old. Fire and light hurt the Draesen, bringing many a strong warrior to slow death, but there were always lines of more coming when a few would fall.

Fog was rolling over the walls like steam from a cauldron, lit a bright yellow by the perilous forest beyond. Darathel still wore the crown, and counted on its magic to preserve the city for their final escape, but he was not his father, and though he had grown up there, he was not the architect of Pelanalda. The crown's bindings in the world were fading as his father faded.

Darathel watched in horror as one of his soldiers was flung from the shieldwall over the line, his blood flying out in every direction. Then he saw what had managed the feat: Katach, flanked by four Draesen even larger than him. They bore immense shields, each one a foot taller than the elves they pushed against, though the warriors wielding them were at least half a head taller than that. Each of them swung a war hammer of heavy iron, turning the head and spike to crush and hook the infantry of the line. Their helms, lacquered black like the armor of the warlord, covered their faces except for the eyes, which caught the mid-day sun and blazed yellow amid dark ashen skin. Katach himself wore a tall helm of similar design, carved on the face to resemble something monstrous. Ivory tusks protruded from his face mask and from a ridge on top of the helm.

They shouted – or sang – in their strange language, moving mercilessly through the defenders, revealing sharp yellow teeth in their wide mouths. Katach swung a great sword, but it did more than cut. Some sort of magic empowered it, and waves of dark air seemed to pulse through the elven formation, striking down soldiers with blindness or madness. As Darathel watched on in horror, the outer wall of the castle suddenly gave way.

The fall was uncanny, for no siege implement provoked it, and it made no sound with its fall, except for at the very end when the rubble bounced. It was as if all the mortar disappeared, all the stones lost their bearing, and fell like gravel poured out onto the earth. The wall, in a way, unmade itself.

"Fall back, my lord!"

Darathel looked to his left and saw Mardrel moving to stand in front of him.

"The whole city will come down if you don't retreat and clear your mind," Mardrel said.

"The city is lost either way," Darathel said. The fall of the wall had created a great confusion among the Draesenith, whether Darathel intended to bring it down or not. Even the emperor and his great warriors were falling back to the rubble, trying to regroup those draesen crushed or scattered by the destructive event.

"I have not lost hope. You shouldn't either. Our people can be recalled," Mardrel said. "Already we are gaining strength."

"Against the emperor... we cannot hold for long."

"Leave that to me and the mages. Go!"

Mardrel pushed his shield against Darathel, and the prince relented. He turned and ran through the ward to the many steps that led to the inner keep. He took them in two leaps and ran inside, scrambling over the fallen doors. In the first great hall were the wounded, being tended to by healers and the herb masters who had not yet passed through the portals at the rear of the city and into the Fay Lands.

He looked quickly for Faedra, but failing to see her among the throng, he moved on, up a spiral staircase and through a branching hallway. At last, he reached the gallery that led to his father's inner sanctum. The statues and tapestries that lined the bright white walls looked dull to his eyes. He took a deep breath and tried to remember them, leaning his psyche on the crown that sat upon his head, a source of chaotic power and ancient memory that searched his thoughts like a god alive.

The shimmering portal to the sanctum withdrew and allowed him passage. He paused. His father's chamber was bare. The bed, table, chairs, screens... everything was missing except the desk. Upon it sat his father's worn pens, dried inkwells and, to Darathel's great surprise, a leather-bound book.

19

"Diorgesh, Diorgesh," Faedra said to herself. Her mind was of two parts – one confused and reeling from the revelation of the ancient void dragon, the other focused intently on the healing magic that would close Tara's wounds. "How do you destroy emptiness?"

"You fill it," Tara said. She lay against a silk pillow on a large bed, breathing laboriously. "I would guess."

"No, no," Faedra said softly. She ran her hands above Tara's ribs, willing them to stitch back together. "Diorgesh represents a..." she shook her head. "How did Katach gain such power?"

"A sacrifice," Tara said. "He sacrificed a high elf, but..."

"But what?"

"It didn't work. Our magic came back when her body was lit on fire."

Tara paused for a moment. "Fire? Are you sure?"

"I saw the altar burn. One of the priests, too. I'll not forget it. It was all I could see from where Ared held me, carrying me away. A bright, violet fire, turning white. Brighter than the sun."

Tara nodded and smiled slightly. "I understand now. One of the other gods took the sacrifice. Fire would have to be... Vulatesh, perhaps?"

"I didn't see a dragon."

"Diorgesh has not shown himself, yet he is at work in the actions of the Draesenith. Of course it could have been Sight herself... either way, that is something hopeful."

"I have a hard time hoping right now."

"Me too, but hope I have. And I can feel time in front of me again."

20

Darathel slowed as he approached the tome. The light from the windows above dimmed, though a few rays continued to fall on the book. Though his focus was on that object, he was also aware that his mind had expanded, and there were thoughts on the margins of his psyche of the whole city, and through them ran tickles of power. He was close to the Fay; the Prim ran across him like water, yet his eyes ignored the power and stared solely at the book.

He pulled out the chair and sat down facing it. It was bound, he saw, in the skin of some sort of reptile. A thought skittered on the outside of his mind that the intricate scales belonged to a dragon, but he did not allow himself to believe it. All the dragons in the world had disappeared or been defeated at the end of the last dominion. Even his father, ancient as he was, could not possess something so rare as dragonhide, nor would he dare to bind a book in the skin of a god.

And yet, he knew that was what it was as he laid his hands upon it. The scales were smooth as polished iron, and just as hard, but warm to the touch like living flesh. The cover was bare except for a jewel of amber set among the scales. It looked like an eye gazing back at him, and Darathel felt that if he were small enough, he could step through it into... something else. He blinked slowly.

THE CROWN OF SIGHT

He opened the cover and beheld his father's handwriting. It was neat and measured, as good as a scribe's, but with the distinctive loops his father had always integrated into his letters. He began to skim the words, and realized it was a history of the city, of the high elves, and of his father. He found a story of his father slaying one of the old dragons after the return of the sun. He flipped far ahead and found stories of his youth, and of his mother. Finally he found the last pages, which were blank.

As he stared at the last few paragraphs, which told of a vain siege of the high elven city of Pelanalda by the savage grey-skinned Draesenith empire, he began to feel a compulsion to pick up a pen and detail what had happened. Something caught his eye, however, as he reached for the pen. He noticed words at the top of the page that mentioned him. He flipped back and found a description of himself and Faedra, and their courtship. It was a courtship that had never happened. Darathel knew they had confessed their hidden feelings just recently, but at the same time, he also knew they were at the end of a long formal courtship.

The words written in his father's book conjured up memories that he knew to be false, though they felt real, and suddenly he understood what his father had been doing. Only his recent memory, of entering the castle and thinking about Faedra, allowed him to know which memory was created, and which was the result of his true history, though that truth was suddenly hard to recall. He dipped the pen in the inkwell and stirred the ink, half-dried and sticky. He took it out and, laying the nib flat, crossed out a sentence mentioning their courtship.

He felt slight nausea as his mind reeled to process it. The memory of their relationship became something else – a dream, half-remembered and missing details. Darathel took a deep breath. He thought of Faedra, and though they had not had the enjoyment of open company the way the book had described, he thought the swift romance the more meaningful. In that moment he gained an understanding of his father, but also of the magic of the crown that sat on his head. Its power was far too vast to allow into the hands of Katach. He closed the book and rose.

He would pass into the Fay Lands and escape with the crown and the book. It was necessary now to take the sacred objects away, though the whole city would fall upon his friends, his subordinates, and his love. Light grew in the windows above. He picked up the book and walked swiftly through the chamber to one of the side-walls.

He held up his hand and the stone there began to crumble, torn apart by vines that grew from the cracks, writhing like dozens of fingers. As the stone fell away, he saw beyond them a vision of the Fay, swimming with the Prim, the magic of creation. It was like a vine-choked forest, sunless and yet full of light, smelling of all the smells of memory. Chaotic, and yet calming.

He stopped. Another presence had disrupted his magic. He watched as the stones, defying time, flew back into place. He tried to exercise his will again, but his connection was dim, almost blurred, and the Fay in his mind seemed dreamlike and unreal.

"There's no escape for you."

Darathel turned to the portal, which blocked the entrance to his father's sanctum. It was shimmering and growing increasingly translucent. He could see a great black figure beyond.

"Katach," Darathel said. He stepped forward as the portal finally died, and he could see the gallery beyond. The entranceway, which was now the last exit to the final portal to the Fay lands, was blocked by the emperor of the Draesenith. The crown seemed to pulse on Darathel's head as the eyes of the grey-skinned giant hardened.

THE CROWN OF SIGHT

"Give me the crown, and I will let you live," Katach said. "You can flee to whatever realms you like."

Darathel narrowed his eyes and steeled himself. "I do not trust the words of those who betray their own oaths."

"You have no choice, boy. You cannot overcome me."

"I have lived a hundred of your lifetimes, mortal." Darathel raised his hand and, feeling the crown speaking to him in some unknown language, unleashed a pillar of fire that rushed toward the emperor. It struck him full on, enveloping him in bright, blinding light.

Then it moved past, the flames dying on Katach's jet-black armor.

"*Old* fool, then," Katach said. "Your pitiful magic does not bind me."

"So that is truly the power of Diorgesh," Darathel said. "Let us test its limits."

Darathel unleashed two more waves of magic, one of light, and one of shimmering darkness. Both fizzled before they reached the Draesen, obeying a silent command as Katach held forth a great gloved hand.

Darathel nodded and drew his sword, an object of pure form in its perfect arc. Immediately he was set upon by two memories – that it at once belonged to his father and was a gift from his mother at the same time. He pushed the thoughts down.

The edge of the sword flashed silver white. He breathed out, feeling the crown cold against his temples, and the blade filled itself with inner light. Opposite him, Katach smiled and drew his own sword, long and with a keen double-edge. It sang slightly as it slid along the copper lip of its scabbard. The Draesen kept the point low, not even raising the blade into a forward guard.

Darathel dashed toward him, slashing and moving through a series of well-practiced arcs. Katach stepped back and turned the strikes with ease, causing light to flash out from the elven blade like flying sparks. His sword rang, but the magic in Darathel's steel did nothing against it. Darathel growled and conjured fire at Katach's feet as he renewed his attack. Green flames leapt up to the Draesen's knees and then died as Katach parried Darathel's two slashes and stepped past the elf's guard.

The long sword's edge slammed against a gap between Darathel's pauldron and breastplate. Pain shattered the connection Darathel maintained to the Fay, and his sword began to sputter and flicker. He refocused his mind, and light suffused the blade again, turning from white to cool blue. He attacked again, and again his magic was nullified. Katach dodged a tight pull cut and kicked at Darathel's knee. Darathel withdrew his forward leg, but not fast enough, and the impact of the blow threw him off balance. Katach quickly stepped forward and lunged single-handed, the wicked tip of his sword breaking mail links under Darathel's left arm and piercing jack and flesh.

The prince winced in pain and staggered back. Katach did not let up, striking two more times at Darathel's armor gaps, breaking mail links and bruising flesh.

"A hundred lifetimes," Katach said as he nimbly turned thrusts and push cuts from Darathel, "but none of them spent in battle. This is barely sport."

Darathel gave a wordless scream and rolled to Katach's left, off-hand. He slashed up and struck under the Draesen's arm. The magic had an effect at last, and the lacquered steel shattered like glass. Pieces fell away, revealing a mail coat beneath, and the emperor even grunted at the surprising pain.

It was a fleeting victory, for as Darathel slid forward to follow through, Katach reached with his left hand and firmly grasped the elf's blade. Darathel twisted and shook, but the grip was like stone. Single-handed, Katach brought his sword down. It crashed against Darathel's helm, then slid over the slick steel to strike the edge of his pauldron. The mail's steel and magic failed, and the sword burst through and cut, stopping at bone. Darathel dropped his sword.

The prince collapsed and rolled away, avoiding a stomp from the giant. He hit a pillar and splayed his legs, hoping to push himself up.

"Stay your hand, Katach!"

To Darathel's surprise, the emperor paused, though the Draesen's fiery eyes remained fixed upon Darathel. The elf realized ice had formed around between him and his opponent, binding Katach's sabatons to the marble floor. With a grunt from the emperor, the ice began to break.

"You cannot bind me," Katach said, chuckling slightly. He turned, and Darathel saw beyond him the small figure of Faedra, her eyes a blazing blue in the white gallery. Beside her stood Tara, a sword held forward in a guard.

"I do not intend to," Faedra said. "Darathel, give him the crown." Her eyes slid past Katach and locked with Darathel's

"No!" Darathel cried, pushing himself to his feet, ignoring the pain that suffused his head and body. He looked down and realized he was bleeding profusely, and it was pooling on the floor. His knees threatened to buckle with the effort.

"Here is my trade, Draesen," Faedra said. "You take the crown, and leave. I have plenty of power left to overcome you."

"If you could kill me, you would," Katach said, grinning.

"It would take me too long to destroy you and to save the life of the prince," Faedra said. "Make your decision now, or prepare yourself for whatever awaits mortals beyond this plane."

Katach hesitated for a moment, glanced at Darathel, and said. "Very well. I will take the crown and leave. You have made your city a poor prize in your haste to destroy me."

"I refuse!" Darathel said, picking up his sword. His arms felt weak, and the rush of battle was giving way to the realization that he was bleeding out. Dying.

"Trust me, my love," Faedra said. "Please trust me."

Darathel stared at her, and though her face was hard, her eyes shimmered and shook, and he lost his will. He leaned against a stone pillar and pulled the golden circlet from his head. As it left contact with his skin, he suddenly felt his legs give out, and he collapsed. His vision swam, and then the gallery was replaced by endless darkness. In the distance, he thought he could hear chimes, but these too seemed to fade.

21

The walls shook. Mortar dust and pebbles rained down. Near the great rear gate of the inner ward, Mardrel commanded the last line of defenders as they tried to evacuate the battlements above. The gate stood open, the largest portal to the Fay Lands. Beyond the stone arches, which lacked the fortifications of the front of the castle, a strange landscape stretched: it was a forest of immense trees, but in the rolling hills beyond and between the trees could be seen windy grasslands under an uncertain sun. It was both familiar and uncanny, and Mardrel had a hard time not looking out into it.

"Sir, the last of the guard are coming down off the battlements now." It was one Mardrel's lieutenants, Garal. "The second squad on the other side of the ward has already reached one of the smaller portals, and we can safely move on without them. Shall we sound the last retreat?"

THE CROWN OF SIGHT

Mardrel nocked an arrow into his longbow. His eyes searched the chaos of the Draesen, who pushed back the shield wall little by little. Behind them he spied, in deep blue-lacquered armor, the enemy commander Saren. They locked eyes for a moment. Mardrel drew and fired, but the commander raised his shield and blocked the shot. Mardrel watched the draesen grin.

"Sir?" the lieutenant said again.

Mardrel glanced at the rear entrance to the keep, secreted among the natural stone base and barely wide enough for one person to walk through. The walls shook again, and a large piece of stone landed between Mardrel and Garal.

"Not yet. Faedra went to fetch the prince. We must hold a little longer."

"How many must we sacrifice in the wait?"

Mardrel gave Garal a hard look. "Until we leave this world behind, we owe him our allegiance. I for one will not brave the heart of dreams as a coward or oath-breaker."

Garal hesitated a moment. "Yes, sir. I'll... We shall hold a while longer. But, sir, how shall we decide-"

"I will decide if our prince is too long in the waiting, and mourn him, and our high mage, dead."

22

Katach smiled as he bent down and picked up the Crown of Sight in his left hand. As if sensing his aspect, its inner light pulsed, and it even emitted a low-pitch resonating hum. Katach could feel it resisting his touch, feel whatever was in it – a mind, a soul – crying in agony at the presence of his flesh. Then, suddenly, the fight stopped, and the crown's light grew constant once again. It hummed now, almost singing, as if accepting its new master.

The emperor sheathed his sword and removed his helm. He tossed it onto the marble floor, then he placed the crown upon his brow. The metal was cold against his skin, chilling his sweat. He felt the crown resist again, pushing against his will.

"Foolish old harpy," Katach said, and drew his sword again. "I'll have your skins and the prince's to pad my throne." He glanced at Darathel, who lay unconscious, clearly struggling to breathe, then turned to the females.

"I think not," Faedra said. "Your god has abandoned you."

Katach narrowed his eyes. His first instinct was to laugh, but something about the calm, almost emotionless blue eyes of the elf gave him pause. He looked down at his feet and saw that ice crystals still clung to his sabatons. He reached for Diorgesh's power and found only the presence of light coming from the circlet of gold.

"I have the crown," Katach said. "That is what matters. And It obeys *me!*" He thrust his hand forward, feeling the crown drawing on some hidden power, fueling him. Fire rolled forward, crackling, only to fail before the feet of Faedra.

"It is not a thing for mortals to possess," Faedra said. "Especially without the protection of the Unbinder. Did you not consider this as you communed with your anti-god? Your nature is divided and can never command the crown, an object of both physical and spiritual existence in one."

Katach snarled and threw his hand forward again, putting all his will against the crown. Instead of fire, what sprang up were leaves and vines, black and twisted. They grew within moments, then died as brambles. He squinted. The elf beyond the dried brambles seemed hard to see, and he realized that the lights overhead were growing dim.

He saw why. The gallery was now held aloft by trees, ugly and twisted. A rain fell from them, hot and of a strange smell. He spat and brought his sword up, intending to charge the elves, but his feet were stuck to the ground. He looked down to see brambles clinging to his ankles. He hacked at them, screaming wordlessly. As he cut each vine, new leaves sprouted, then died, and with each cut the bramble crawled a little further up his legs.

Desperate, he reached up to take the crown off. He found it impossible to remove. His own hands resisted the motion, and the circlet sang in his ears as it clung there. He could even feel it boring into him, somehow, parting his flesh. There was a deeper horror to it as well, and as he struggled against it he could feel some piece of his inner soul welcoming it in. The crown truly had its own will, and he could almost hear it speaking in tones and chimes rather than words.

He looked around and found the gallery gone, replaced by a forest of twisted trees and choking vines. The image of the elf hovered in front of his face, moving past him, somehow unaffected by the dark world that surrounded him.

"Help!" he choked out.

"I cannot," Faedra said.

Katach felt his breath shortening, then slowing. His heart seemed to slow as well. He felt himself sitting down, on something right and comfortable.

A throne. He looked at his hands. The gauntlets that covered them were gone, rusted and rotted away to reveal smooth, grey skin. Mail links were falling away from his arms. His sword was gone – to where he could not guess. Infusing him was a calming presence, and he leaned back. He wondered at what he was seeing.

What were these things? How did they change so? Where was the light? What was the light?

Sleep felt heavy on his lids along with a feeling of satisfaction and greatness.

He was the emperor. He was the ruler of the world.

The last thought of his own self – the self that existed before he had placed the crown on his head – was a wondering why Diorgesh had left him, and he remembered a failed sacrifice, with hot, sickening blood on his tongue. In place of the Unbinder was another dragon, coming toward him as if called by the crown. His mortal mind was terrified by it, but his soul begged for its presence.

Then he slept.

23

Faedra held back Tara for a moment. Together they watched the walls fall away and the light of the Fay lands envelope the room. Katach, emperor of the Draesenith, was in a trance, his eyes seeing nothing.

"Step wide," she said to Tara. Together they walked around the mumbling mortal to where Darathel lay on the ground. He was barely breathing.

"He lives," Tara said.

"Not for long," Faedra said. "Without the crown to sustain him..."

With strength impossible for her diminutive size, she knelt down and scooped him up into her arms.

"Lady-" Tara said, shock on her cold face.

"Quickly, I must take him to the Fay, where he can heal."

"The Fay Lands are there," Tara said, pointing to where Katach now sat. Vines were creeping over the ensorcelled mortal, and yet he still mumbled wordlessly.

"That could take us to the mortal's dream, and I dare not tread there. Come, you must help me reach the back door."

Tara nodded and followed Faedra out of the gallery and to one of the halls. On the threshold, Tara stopped and looked back into the gallery.

"What is it?" Faedra said.

"Nothing that matters," Tara said, and turned away.

They passed two Draesen, who jumped in surprise as they saw them. Tara leapt in front of Faedra and dispatched one of the enemies, who disturbingly did not even raise his sword in defense. The other, a massive draesen that towered above the two elves, turned and ran toward the center of the keep, abandoning his massive shield and Warhammer.

"No time to wonder," Faedra said, and stepped over the dead enemy, racing down a now dark gallery of marble and stone.

24

Saren raised his shield and squinted his eyes shut. The wave of fire flowed over the it, the flames licking his neck. The back of his hand began to feel hot, and he could smell the acrid scent of charred leather. He forced his eyes open to see his gauntlets and the straps on his shield smoking. He threw down the great steel kite and dropped his sword. With a quick tug he removed his gauntlet and threw it on the ground, just as the back of his hand began to burn.

He looked around himself, and saw his front line collapsing backwards, running from the waves of deadly magic coming from the last, desperate stand of the elves. The warriors of the shieldwall, once brave and deadly, were cowering, screaming, falling, dying.

"You bloody cowards!" he screamed as the rout pressed against the pikemen of the rear lines, who refused to turn. Saren reached down for his sword and raised his arm against another wave of magic – something more than fire. He watched one of Katach's elites collapse beside him, his eyes charred holes. In response, one of the Draesenith mages returned a bolt of magic. Elves ducked and dove out of the way. It was the first time he had seen one of his mages put themselves to use in the battle.

"Reform at the gate!" He shouted. He repeated it to the sergeants as he stepped back toward the ruined castle gate, hopping over dead bodies of friend and foe. The pikemen obeyed immediately, and soon the infantry of the forward lines fell back into formation. Saren could see that in places, warriors were unable or unwilling to get back into line, and he spat on the ground.

"Sir!"

Saren turned and saw one of Katach's elites, his armor singed and dented in many places. He held a nervous salute.

"Where is the emperor?" Saren said.

"He... something happened to him." The warrior removed his helm, and his face was full of doubt and fear. "He disappeared. Into the cursed world. He was... wearing the crown when I saw him last."

"The Fay?" Saren said. "It took him?"

"Yes, sir."

"I understand now." He jumped on a nearby stone and began shouting. "Fall back! Fall back to the second wall! Fall back I say!" He jumped down and stepped over to two sergeants, who looked bewildered. "Take your squads in a retreat to the second city wall, or what's left of it. Join the archers there. Our protection against the elven mages is lost this day."

"What about the emperor?" one of the sergeants said.

"He's gone," said the elite warrior, who still stood beside Saren. "The Great Dragon has betrayed us!"

Saren nodded toward the warrior. "I'm not spending lives to buy something that is gone forever, especially now that Katach's god has abandoned us. We'll fall back and hold against the elves, regroup, and crush who chooses to remain. I want no more dead lions. Go!"

25

Faedra carried Darathel down a narrow, dark stair, with Tara close behind. They reached the hidden rear entrance at the bottom landing; Tara raised a set of bars and pushed open the door. Outside, in the sun, they saw what remained of the city guard amassed outside the great gate to the Fay Lands. Faedra, still carrying Darathel, padded across the empty space of the wards toward where Mardrel stood, leaning on a spear.

"We are here!" Faedra said. "Begin the last retreat."

"There may be no need, my lady," Mardrel said. "The enemy is in a rout."

"How?"

"I know not why, but our magic suddenly became more deadly. The Draesenith became deathly afraid of it and many of their warriors bolted. The enemy general seemed unable to bring them back in line."

Tara said, "They will certainly regroup. They are an army, after all, and their last general is said to be their most resourceful."

"I agree," Faedra said. "We must continue to evacuate."

Mardrel paused, gazing upon Darathel. "Where is the crown?"

"Gone," Faedra said. "Katach tried to use it, but as I suspected it is not something mortals may possess in the normal course of things. It drew his… soul, that separate essence mortals have, away to the Eternal Dream."

"If the crown is gone, how is the city still standing?"

Faedra lay the prince down on the ground and found the book, still tucked into a bag at Darathel's waist.

"This," she said. "It is our history, imperfect as it is. Do you have any way to escape the city without going into the Fay?"

"I do, now that the enemy is in retreat," Mardrel said. "The hidden gates will be accessible again."

"Take it, then," Faedra said, handing the book to the captain. "I don't know what traversing the Fay Lands may do to it, so keep it safe here in the world-that-is, if you can. Flee, and tell your soldiers to hold no longer to this stack of stone."

"As you wish, lady."

Faedra ran her hand over Darathel's forehead. His eyes flicked open for a moment, then closed. "I must take him away. He can heal in the Fay."

"Farewell, then," Mardrel said. "If we meet again, I will return the book."

"I expect you to. Tara?"

"I shall come with you," Tara said. "Though Pelanalda was my home, I am bound to serve my king."

"The king is gone."

"He lies upon the ground."

"Help me up, then," Faedra said, putting her arms under Darathel. "The strength I drew on is waning."

Tara knelt down on the other side of Darathel. Together, she and Faedra lifted him and carried him toward the gate. As they passed under the stone arches, the light and sound around them changed. Colors became sharper, sound clearer. There was no sun under the canopy of leaves, but it was light and cool. They moved quickly, and the trees almost raced by. When they looked back, the city was far distant, a shining white monument in perfect relief, with no sign of destruction.

"There is no going back now, is there?" Tara said.

"The way out is forward," Faedra said.

Darathel opened his eyes and gazed at Faedra. They stopped and laid him down on a bed of leaves. The wind blew, and it carried the sound of birds. Day grew above them, wrig-

THE CROWN OF SIGHT

gling through gaps in the leaves to make spots of light on the ground. The wind carried a fresh scent, like rain on new grass.

"Where are we?" he said.

"Safe, my love." Faedra touched his face lightly.

"My father's book," he said, reaching to his hip.

"That, too, is safe."

Darathel leaned back into Tara's arms as she laid him flat, his eyes focused on Faedra. "Good. Things will be remembered as he wished them to be. Me? I prefer to remember things as they really were. You cannot have bravery without despair."

"Most of the people escaped. They will remember the valor of Pelanel and his people." Faedra knelt down lifted his head. Her hands passed painlessly over his wounds. Light fell from lips with her breath.

"You do not understand the power of that book. It will be as my father has written it. The past is memory, and memory is written."

"It is good that the power has passed away, then," Faedra said. "The power to remove one's mistakes is tempting." Her hands moved from his chest up to his face, and she pushed away his hair. "I would dearly like to be free of the regret of loving you so long in doubt."

"Faedra, my love… You are altogether better this way, though I would like it if you stopped crying." He reached up and touched a tear that was forming at the corner of Faedra's eye.

"I don't believe I can. You will have to accept it. Rest now. I will be here. I will always be here with you."

Darathel nodded and closed his eyes.

The End

About the Author

David Van Dyke Stewart is an author, musician, YouTuber, and educator who currently lives in California with his wife and children. He received his musical education as a student of legendary flamenco guitarist Juan Serrano and spent the majority of his 20s as a performer and teacher in California and Nevada before turning his attention to writing fiction, an even older passion than music. He is the author of *Muramasa: Blood Drinker, Water of Awakening*, the *Needle Ash* series, and *Prophet of the Godseed*, as well as numerous novellas, essays, and short stories.

You can find his YouTube channel at http://www.youtube.com/rpmfidel where he creates content on music education, literary analysis, movie analysis, philosophy, and logic.

Sign up to his mailing list at http://dvspress.com/list for a free book and advance access to future projects. You can email any questions or concerns to stu@dvspress.com.

Be sure to check http://davidvstewart.com and http://dvspress.com for news and free samples of all his books.

Made in the USA
Lexington, KY
15 July 2019